THE SAME CITY

THE SAME CITY

LUISGÉ MARTÍN

Translated from the Spanish by
Tomasz Dukanovich

HB Hispabooks
Publishing

Hispabooks Publishing, S. L.
Madrid, Spain
www.hispabooks.com

English translation of Cavafy's poem "The City" by Edmund Keeley
 and Philip Sherrard. *Collected Poems,* by C. P. Cavafy, edited by George
 Savidis. Revised Edition. Princeton University Press, 1992.

Originally published in Spain as *La misma ciudad* by Anagrama, 2013
First published in English by Hispabooks, 2015
English translation copyright © by Tomasz Dukanovich
Copy-editing by Cecilia Ross
Design © Simonpates - www.patesy.com

ISBN 978-84-943496-8-3 (trade paperback)
ISBN 978-84-943496-9-0 (ebook)
Legal Deposit: M-6009-2015

Esta obra ha sido publicada con una subvención
del Ministerio de Educación, Cultura y Deporte de España

For Antonio Prol,
For the everlasting debt of affection

Sky, not spirit, do they change,
those who cross the sea.

HORACE

Without stirring abroad
One can know the whole world;
Without looking out of the window
One can see the way of heaven.
The further one goes,
The less one knows.

Tao Te Ching, 47

Almost all schools of psychology, from classic psychoanalysis through to Gestalt psychotherapy, concern themselves with that melancholic or despairing state of mind that usually rears its head in people approaching the halfway point in life, that state which in somewhat unscientific vernacular we are in the habit of calling the "midlife crisis." At approximately forty years old, human beings cast their minds back, recall the dreams they had when they were young, then take stock of their achievements since that time and the possibilities they still have of attaining the wonderful life they had imagined. The result is always distressing. The man who had dreamed of being a movie star, for example, often finds himself performing slapstick at children's parties or doing commercials. And if by chance, through talent or sheer luck, he has managed to end up starring in films and has become an idol of the masses, thus fulfilling his aspirations, he immediately discovers some disadvantage or major downside to the profession—the servitude of fame, the frivolousness of artistic circles, or the envy of other actors—that casts a shadow over his victory. The man who had imagined he would experience passionate relationships and powerful emotions sooner or later becomes acquainted with betrayal, cheating, loathing, or, more commonly, tedium. And the man who had thought that at least he would always possess youthful vigor and enthusiasm is suddenly struck down by sickness or sees death looming imminently before him. Life, in reality, is a nightmarish trance, and when we reach that taciturn season of middle age, at forty or forty-five, we understand with acute clarity that it is also too short, just as we always used to hear our parents or elderly people say, and that as a result, it doesn't give any of us time to put right the mistakes we made or to set sail on courses different from the ones that were decided upon at some point in the past.

At this crucial and sensitive age, we usually think we've made a mess of everything we've done. We come to believe that the lack of enthusiasm with which we approach our work, the nonchalant or lukewarm composure with which we love our spouse or our children, and the apathy that we feel toward almost everything that used to stir up excitement in us are the result of our errors and not the irreparable consequence of the years that have gone by. Contrarily, other people's lives seem to be ever more remarkable. We look around ourselves and always come upon people who live in houses like the ones we would love to own if only we had the money to buy them, friends who hobnob in the social circles we would relish joining, work colleagues who still love their spouses with a fiery passion we aren't even able to remember anymore, and neighbors who travel to some faraway, idyllic corner of the planet every three months to visit its temples or beaches. If they are similar in age to us, those same people look at us in turn with corresponding envy and think that we're happy because we have time to read the books that are piling up and gathering dust on their own shelves, because we do undemanding jobs, or because almost without lifting a finger, we have women falling at our feet. What is more, sometimes the causes of the envy are identical— we want from the lives of others what they want from ours. In short, at the age of forty, happiness becomes an issue that only pertains to other people.

I met Brandon Moy at a writers' congress held in Cuernavaca in March 2008 and then developed quite a close rapport with him when he moved to Madrid in spring the following year. He was born in the Brooklyn area of New York in 1960 and from a young age had been a successful man. He'd graduated from Columbia University with flying colors, immediately afterward started working at a prestigious law firm, and married a girl he was madly in love with. Before turning thirty, he was renting an apartment in Lower Manhattan, where he'd always dreamed of living, and had fathered a child.

From that moment, his life was untroubled. Thanks to his professional reputation, he was able to change jobs three times and achieve a comfortable financial position. With the inheritance from his father-in-law, who had died in an accident, he and his wife decided to move to a more spacious apartment, beside Central Park, and later, in 1999, they bought a small vacation home on Long Island. They tried to have another child before age took its toll on his wife's body, but were unable to do so. Instead, they bought a Mastiff puppy that

grew a few months later into a giant and deaf-
ened the household with its barking. With that,
Moy's life quickly became a serene, banal pas-
sage of time. He had almost everything a man
in his position could wish for, but now that he
had acquired it all, he was doubtful as to what
the benefits actually were. He loved Adriana,
his wife, and never had any embarrassing arguments with her, but he often got bored when
they were together, so if they went out for
dinner or to the theater, he did everything possible to ensure that other husband-and-wife
friends accompanied them. The love he felt for
his son Brent was even greater and somewhat
strange, one might say atavistic, but despite that,
he couldn't help reflecting sometimes that in
order to take care of him, he'd had to sacrifice
many of the activities that used to make him
happy when he was young. When Brent was
born, he and Adriana stopped going to parties
and clubs, the tent they used to take with them
on weekend getaways to the Catskill Mountains
near New York was stored away, and they can-
celed the plans they had made to travel around
the parts of Europe they had never visited, and
the south of India, to which, having a hippy
older brother, he had always dreamed of making a pilgrimage. He didn't find his job, which

involved resolving legal matters for a financial services company, fulfilling anymore, and in his eyes the boss he had to work under had, over the years, turned into a kind of bloodthirsty, dimwitted ogre who tormented him. To achieve professional success and make a killing with his career in law, he had long since given up his literary activities, which had been his greatest passion during his college years, when he met Adriana. He had also been gradually losing interest in his hobbies; he no longer played the saxophone, except on occasion at some special, formal event when asked to do so, or took part in the meetings of a Brooklyn political debate society of which he was a member. So his life now consisted only of experiences devoid of sensation, and comfortable routines.

Every Monday, when he left the office, he went to a heated swimming pool on West 51st Street and swam for almost two hours to loosen his muscles, which, after the inactivity of the weekend, were usually stiff and painful. Then he walked home, ate dinner with Adriana, and lay down to read a book until he fell asleep. On Monday, September 10, 2001, he had to go to a litigator's office for an emergency meeting that ran considerably late, but despite that, he went to the pool and swam for two hours as always, until the thoughts disappeared from his mind and, exhausted by the effort, his body felt soothed. It was later than usual, but he didn't want to take a cab home. He called Adriana to let her know he wasn't going to arrive at the normal time and calmly headed north along Lexington Avenue and then along 60th Street, where he lived. This route, which he took every Monday, though at a slightly earlier hour, took him past the Continental restaurant, which at that time was apparently one of the most highly regarded restaurants in the city, or at least it had an exclusive reputation among a particular group of elegant, trendy clients. When I traveled to New York in June 2011, I walked along those streets, following the route Brandon Moy took, and I looked for the Continental, to see what it was like, but it was no longer there. According to Moy, who had never actually gone in, the premises had two wide, bare windows on both sides of the doorway, and one could gaze through them at the diners reveling inside. The light was dim, and the atmosphere, despite the pervading air of formality, always seemed lively and festive. Sometimes, when passing by, Moy had thought he could take Adriana there as a surprise, but then he never found the occasion to do it.

That day, when he was on his way home, some of the customers were already finishing their dinners. Moy stopped for an instant at the window, glanced inside absent-mindedly, and saw one of his best friends from his teenage years standing beside one of the tables. He hadn't heard from him since he'd been expelled from college in his first year, at the age of twenty, for being too rebellious and bohemian.

Moy stood there, disturbed, watching him, and suddenly recalled the dreams they had nurtured together, the afternoons lost in conversation or philosophical debates, the girls they had shared, the almost mystic visions they would relate to each other when they experimented with drugs, the science fiction tales they wrote together, and the midnight baseball games they played with a group of classmates at a field in Brooklyn. He felt a slight chill and a sudden desire to cry for everything that had been falling into ruin since that time.

His friend, whose name was Albert Fergus, was standing close to the door and holding open the overcoat of the woman who was with him. She had just risen from the table and was laughing at something Fergus had said. He carried on talking eloquently, pulling faces and gesturing as though he were cheering someone on. While the woman donned her overcoat and was putting some things away in her purse, Brandon Moy gazed at them, hypnotized, from the street. The image of the restaurant as seen through the window was like a silent movie. What the customers were saying, the hubbub, and the music playing inside could not be heard. Therefore the only way to interpret what was happening was by observing gestures, body language, and the décor of the premises, and with that mix of ingredients, everything always seems wonderful. Moy examined the characters' cheerful expressions and imagined that the words they were saying were full of emotion and importance. In the time it took for Albert Fergus and his companion to head toward the restaurant door and step out into the street, Brandon Moy had already fantasized a complete reconstruction of his old friend's life.

When Fergus saw him there, on the sidewalk, he hugged him excitedly. His eyes were gleaming, as though he, too, felt the desire to cry. Almost without stopping for breath, he told Moy everything that had happened since those college years when they'd stopped seeing each other. He'd traveled around the

United States and Mexico for several months, experimented with hallucinogenic drugs, lived among native people and beautiful women, spent some time in a desert cave, joined a commune of Buddhist monks in San Diego, and worked as a boxer to pay off some debts he'd accumulated. He'd continued to write science fiction stories in these notebooks he always carried around with him, and one day, quite by chance, one of the executives of a production company who worked for Metro Goldwyn Mayer read them. He was offered a job as a scriptwriter in Hollywood and moved to Los Angeles, where he'd lived ever since. Over the years, he'd given up writing. Now he was responsible for coordinating scriptwriters on a few successful television series and scouting for young talent. He'd been married, but his marriage had gotten stuck in a few mires, and they had to divorce. Then he'd had various romantic relationships, some more serious than others, although he preferred—he said with childish mischievousness—the chaotic, single life. Then he introduced Moy to Tracy, who remained at his side, listening to his words in amusement.

"I'm the one who makes his life in New York chaotic," she said, laughing.

Brandon Moy studied Fergus that whole time with a vacant, wistful expression, as if all the phenomena being described to him were playing out before his very eyes. Suddenly, he experienced a feeling of unbridled admiration for Fergus, like that felt by small children for their parents or their teachers. While he listened to him, his attention was drawn to the details of his attire—the cashmere suit, its straight cut conforming to the demands of fashion; the steel watch with the dark strap; the highly polished, pointy-toed shoes; the rounded belt buckle; the green-framed glasses; the thick, copper ring; the loose tie. He thought it was possible to see the outlines of his old friend's life in all those elements, the hallmarks of his adventures or of the prestige he had achieved.

"And you?" asked Fergus, "What's been going on in your life these past years?"

Brandon Moy felt ashamed of himself and stammered a few incomprehensible words. Then he gave a toothy smile, an obsequious, sickly sweet expression that Fergus pretended not to see.

"I bet you also have plenty of women making your life chaotic!" Tracy interjected to try and distract from the situation, which had become embarrassing.

"Only one," explained Moy, without keeping the joke running. "I married Adriana. You met her," he said to Fergus, who screwed up his eyes as though he were trying to remember.

"The girl with the blue teeth," Moy added to prompt his memory.

"The girl with the blue teeth," Fergus repeated. "And you're still married to her?"

Brandon Moy nodded, averting his eyes and staring at the ground, as though the acknowledgement were humiliating. At that moment, Fergus looked at his watch and apologized, because that very night he had to catch a plane to Boston, where he had an appointment with a drama screenwriter to revise some scenes for his next movie, before traveling the following day to Los Angeles.

"I don't sleep much," he said to Moy as he embraced him, "but I'll have time to sleep when I'm dead."

They said a hurried goodbye, exchanged business cards, and arranged to have dinner together when Fergus came back to New York for a meeting with his producer two or three weeks later. Moy waited until Fergus got into the taxi that Tracy had flagged down and then stood there motionless for a long time, staring at the end of the street, the traffic lights, and the black sky with the same dumbfounded expression.

As he sullenly resumed his journey home, he remembered everything that Fergus had told him about his life, but regarding every one of those events, he pictured only pleasurable and joyful moments. Thinking about his journeys around the United States and Mexico, he imagined the stunning scenery; about his time spent living with natives, the folk dances; about the boxing matches, the glory of his great victories; about his days in the desert cave, the inner peace nature gives us; about the beautiful women he had been with, the nights of wild sex; about his experiences with drugs, the celestial, psychedelic visions; and about his work as a scriptwriter, he considered only the creative allure and the glamour of cinema. As psychologists would rightly observe, Moy did not think about any of the painful, sad, or disastrous moments that had also formed part of those adventures. It did not occur to him to envisage the eternal afternoons of boredom he would have spent traveling straight, barren roads, or the humiliation he must have felt when the blow of an opponent knocked him to the mat in front of a rowdy audience, or the biting cold that would have frozen him to the bone during the nights in the desert, or the hunger or the fear of those days spent in the open air, the vulnerability he had to have felt waking up in the mornings without a woman at his side, or the sense of estrangement he would have experienced when betraying his creative spirit by writing shallow dialogues for teen flicks. Not one of those images crossed Brandon Moy's mind as he recreated the fabulous life of Fergus in his imagination. He didn't imagine a single moment of misfortune.

On the other hand, his own life struck him as consisting of a host of trifling events, instances of modest self-denial and humiliation that were gradually extinguishing it. For example, he remembered the Bob Inkalis concert he hadn't been able to go to the week before because Adriana had felt tired at the last minute. Bob Inkalis was a legendary saxophonist who had started to perform at the very beginning of his career with Art Blakey and Bill Evans. In the early eighties, he'd made some memorable albums and done a countrywide tour. Moy had gone to two of his concerts, and at one of them he'd tried to get backstage to express his admiration. Then Inkalis had plunged into the abyss of drugs and alcohol. Since then, he hadn't recorded anything or performed on stage. When

Moy had found out he was going to give a concert in Madison Square Garden, he felt a childlike sense of excitement. He immediately bought tickets and spent several days listening to old recordings he had of his. But on the day of the concert, Adriana, who had forgotten the date, arrived home exhausted. Moy, ready to go out, was waiting impatiently for her. She collapsed into the armchair beside him and looked at him imploringly.

"I don't have the strength to go and be stuck in a crowd," she breathed. She rested her head on his shoulder, closed her eyes, and whispered tenderly, "You go. You like Ginkali so much, and you shouldn't miss out because of me." Then she fell asleep.

It irritated Moy that she hadn't even remembered the musician's name correctly, but he didn't stir from her side. He began thinking that Bob Inkalis would probably give another concert soon. Or that so many years later, his lungs destroyed as a result of fast living, his saxophone would sound like wheezing puffs of air, a crackling rasp, and in that case it was better never to see him again, so as not to cast a shadow over the memories he had of him.

He didn't get angry with Adriana over what had happened, but he felt that yet again his life had been drained of its meaningfulness, that prophecies could be made about it that would always be fulfilled. It was a diffuse, acerbic anxiety, like that which one sometimes feels when thinking about one's own death.

When Moy got home that night after running into Albert Fergus, Adriana was putting Brent to bed. He chatted with his son for a few minutes and then went to the kitchen to make something for dinner.

"Do you remember how when you were young, you used to paint your lips blue?" he asked Adriana while rummaging in the fridge.

The remark made her laugh, and she got up to help him.

"When I was young, I did a lot of crazy stuff," she said. Then she stood still, as if pondering something, and gave a mischievous pout. "So, I'm not young anymore?"

Moy began to chop vegetables.

"The day I met you, they were painted blue, but the lipstick had stuck to your teeth, so they were blue, too. It was like you had magic teeth. Or some sort of festering gum disease," he added, smiling. "I never told you, because I didn't want to embarrass you. But from that day on, my friends and I always called you 'the girl with the blue teeth.'"

Adriana embraced Moy from behind as he continued chopping vegetables and placed them in a bowl to season them.

"What made you think of that just now?" she asked warmly. "Do my teeth look blue?"

Moy shrugged his shoulders and stood motionless beside her, without saying a word and unsure whether the feeling flooding through him was sadness or resentment. In a vague, inscrutable way, he thought his own failure was Fergus's fault. Then, turning around, he parted Adriana's lips with one finger and touched her teeth as though he were trying to turn them blue again.

That night he ate dinner silently in front of the television and pretended he had to finish a piece of work on the computer, so he wouldn't have to make conversation with Adriana. When she went to bed, a little before midnight, Moy turned off all the lights in the house and sat in an armchair near the window. He once again recalled the desires he'd had when he was young, the great marvels he had expected from life. Outside he could see the lights of Manhattan, and he began to cry. He had just turned forty-one. He had not yet seen any of the dreams he thought he held dear come to fruition, and he probably never would; at his age, he would no longer have the opportunity to do the kinds of things Fergus had described to him. He wouldn't be able to sleep in caves anymore, experiment with drugs, or go back-packing to faraway cities. The time when his life had not been a foregone conclusion had now slipped away.

Before going into the bedroom, he had a whisky and took a sleeping pill, but despite that, it took him a long time to get to sleep. He tried to think about pleasant, calm things. About Adriana, whom he could hear breathing by his side. About his son, Brent, who had already begun acting like a young man. About the Manhattan skyline that could be seen from Brooklyn at night. About the Long Island house. At four in the morning, he finally fell asleep. It was deep and peaceful, as if none of the concerns that had unsettled him during the day were really of any importance.

Adriana woke him, as she did every day, at six thirty in the morning, after stepping out of the shower. She woke him again at seven, but Moy wasn't able to rouse himself. At seven twenty, when, as always, she was going to take their son to school on her way to work, she went into the bedroom again and shook him until he sat up in bed and opened his eyes. She informed him that breakfast was ready in the kitchen and that he would be late for work if he didn't hurry.

Brandon Moy later remembered all his movements that morning very precisely. He idled away a few more minutes in bed, then got up feeling stiff and lethargic and had a lazy breakfast. At about eight, he shaved and took a shower, standing under the stream of boiling water until it woke him up. He took his time choosing a suit and then found a tie he hadn't worn for some time. Finally, when he was fully dressed, he put his laptop into his briefcase and gathered up some papers he had littered on the dining table and might need in one of that day's meetings. He didn't look at his watch, but he must have left home between eight thirty and twenty to nine. Nobody saw him. He walked toward the newsstand where he usually bought the *New York Times* and the *Wall Street Journal* every morning, but before reaching it, he realized he only had hundred dollar bills, so he detoured down 59th Street, where the entrance to the subway he caught every morning was situated. Just before going in, he heard the blast—a muffled, dry, cracking thunderclap, as though metal or glass were being torn apart. He stopped for a moment and looked around, searching for the cause of the noise, but couldn't see anything. Beside him, an old lady taking a walk came to a standstill on the sidewalk and looked up toward the sky, to the rooftops. A startled woman dropped the cup of coffee she was holding, and it rolled along the sidewalk into a gutter. Everyone was alarmed for a split second, and then continued on their way. Moy went the rest of the way down the subway stairs, passed through a turnstile, and caught the first southbound train, following the route he took everyday. But two stations later, on 42nd Street, the train engines ground to a halt, and a staff member rushed through the carriages forcing all the passengers to get off. "A small airplane's crashed into one of the World Trade Center towers," Moy heard a man on the platform saying. "All communications have been cut off in the area." Moy felt dizzy, his eyes closed. Robertson & Millyander, the financial services agency he'd worked at for over seven years, had its headquarters on the ninety-sixth floor of the North Tower. From his small, badly ventilated office, you could see the labyrinthine streets of the city, the grayish water of the Hudson, and the New Jersey coast. He went up to the man who had just announced the accident, to listen to his explanations, but amid the uproar of all the passengers, he couldn't hear anything. He passed through the throng on the platform in a matter of seconds, like a sleepwalker, and then came out onto the street with the intention of catching a cab south.

Every single person can remember what he or she was doing when they learned that the Twin Towers in New York had been attacked. It's one of those crucial moments that, because of their brutality or consequences, remain branded in our memories. I'd gone to have lunch at my parents' house and was watching the news with them. The broadcast opened with the images of the first plane—a light aircraft, according to the newscaster, whose explanation on this point coincided with that of the man on the platform—crashing into the tower. My sister was at a swimming class and sensed how everyone swimming around her suddenly began to head toward the sides and climb out of the pool. I heard about a woman, a friend of a friend of mine, who was caught in bed with a lover because her husband, who never went home for lunch, returned that day to watch the excruciating images on television with her. I even met a writer who had shut himself away in a country house in the Sierra de Cazorla to finish writing a novel and heard nothing about the incident until September

13th. Brandon Moy, who worked in the building the first plane crashed into and who should have been in his office at that time, as he was every day, remembered with almost scientific precision everything that happened that morning. His twenty-seven colleagues at Robertson & Millyander died in the attack. He didn't die, but his life changed radically over the course of those hours.

When he got above ground again, the columns of smoke rising toward the sky could be seen from every angle of New York. The traffic had stopped, and the roads were full of people staring up bewilderedly at the skyline, astonished by a spectacle they could not yet comprehend. Moy heard a woman say that the plane had gone through both towers, but shortly afterward, in one of the noisy huddles that was forming on the sidewalks, he found a young man wearing headphones who was repeating out loud what he was hearing on the radio— it wasn't one plane but two that had crashed into the towers, which were now ablaze. There were thousands of people trapped inside. It was impossible to calculate the number of victims at that point, but all the plane passengers and many of the World Trade Center workers would no doubt have been pulverized in the collision. It was approximately nine thirty in the morning, and none of the plans that later began to obsess Moy had crossed his mind yet, so he tried to call his wife so she wouldn't worry. But the lines were down, and he couldn't get through to her. That fact—a technological limitation, a chance occurrence—determined the rest of his life.

Brandon Moy walked for more than an hour toward Lower Manhattan. The police stopped him from entering the area around the World Trade Center, as they were doing with everyone there on foot, so he stood behind a trench of vehicles and unfamiliar machinery and watched the cloud of fire that was darkening the air, the shadow of burning skyscrapers. He heard the resounding boom when the towers fell. He saw men with bleeding head wounds, or tourniquets on different parts of their bodies, going past him. He spent a while clasping a woman with burns on the skin of her thighs and belly. He observed the shocked or crazed expressions on the faces of the people coming from downtown, all of them covered with ash. The taste of cinders, of scorched air, clung to his palate. And he joined a medical team to help undress victims with open wounds who were waiting to be treated. He spent over five hours in that place, between Canal and Chambers, and although he didn't speak to anyone for several months about what he had seen there, it all came back to him later with disturbing accuracy.

The first time it crossed his mind that this disastrous moment could be the last opportunity he would have in his life to do everything he had never dared to do—sleep in caves, take drugs, write poems—was at midday, when he tried to call Adriana again to tell her he was alive. The lines were still down, overwhelmed by the massive overload. More than three hours had passed since the first plane had crashed into the tower in which he worked, so his wife, child, parents, and everyone who knew him would be thinking that he had died. They would be thinking that his body had been destroyed in the explosion from the collision, that he'd flung himself out of the building to escape from the fire, or that while still alive, he had plunged into the ground along with the building's steel frame and was now lying cut to pieces among the rubble and the waste. Everyone would be sure by this point that Brandon Moy no longer existed. That he was now a piece of detritus or charred clay. "The dust with which God made man in Genesis," he would say later when talking about it. "The dust that goes back to being only dust when everything is over. Filthy sludge, dregs."

Since waking up that morning, Moy had not thought about his encounter with Albert Fergus again, but suddenly, among the crowd, he saw a woman coming toward him staring hard, and she reminded him of Tracy. The woman, just like her, wore a fine, woolen overcoat, with huge, fifties-style lapels. It was jade green but covered in hot, black ash. When she reached him, she collapsed. Moy knelt down beside her, slid his arm around her back, and slapped her in the face to revive her. The woman, however, did not respond. Moy then did something strange that he never managed to fully understand. He bent forward to kiss her on the lips. He separated them with his fingertips and then pressed his tongue to her gums, which tasted of ash. Months later, when he remembered that bizarre, moving event, he came to believe that he was trying, like in children's stories, to bring her back to life. But in reality it was only an act of emancipation, the first time he had broken the rules in many years. That woman, ugly and disfigured from the damage she had suffered in the catastrophe, had reminded him of Tracy, and Moy, like Fergus, wanted to kiss her, to feel the freedom one feels when one doesn't owe loyalty to anybody.

He picked the woman up, putting his other arm under her knees, and carried her to the first-aid station. He left her there lying on the hood of a car. At that moment, he became aware of everything that was happening. He realized that probably nobody thought he was alive any more, and then he suddenly recalled Albert Fergus's laughter as he draped the coat with the huge lapels on Tracy in the restaurant, his worldly and confident air, and all his adventures, which despite lacking the gloss of detail, because they had been recounted hurriedly in the street, seemed thrilling. When they'd said goodbye on the sidewalk, while he was watching the taxi pull away, he'd thought that if he could be reborn, he would like to live like Fergus, with that scatterbrained impetuosity. And now, only a few hours later, Providence was offering him the chance to be born again. Death is a biological act, a failure of the vital organs of the body, but it can also be, as the poets say, a spiritual state, or an attitude. Brandon Moy thought that morning, as he gazed at the spectral figures around him, that if none of the people who knew him thought at that moment that he was alive, it was in his hands to decide whether he really was. He would never have dared to leave his wife and child under normal circumstances, but that day, while bandaging wounds and moistening the lips of dying men with damp cloths at the first-aid station, he began to feel that for the first time in ages, he had no commitment to them. After almost fifteen years of marriage, he was still in love with Adriana, but with a very different passion from the one he had felt when he was young. He no longer experienced hot flashes or went weak at the knees when he thought about her or imagined himself being deserted or widowed. When he embraced her, he no longer felt fevered excitement but instead calm. He wanted to continue living with her, but for a long time he hadn't been able to understand why. "It's possible that we sometimes carry on living with someone for fear of destroying the past and not out of a desire to build a future with them," Brandon Moy once said to me. "I think that's what happened to me with Adriana. I never considered leaving her, because that would've been like acknowledging that we'd failed and that those dreams we'd had for so many years were no more than smoke or pretense. Adriana wouldn't have been able to take it if I'd left and met other women. She couldn't have resigned herself to me living nearby, in another neighborhood in New York, and now and again going to the restaurants we'd gone to together. She would've hated me for all that. And I would've felt guilt and shame. Leaving someone is a betrayal. Dying, on the other hand, is not."

That was the enigma, or sophism, that Brandon Moy came up with that morning to justify his actions; if he had announced to his wife one day that he was leaving her to travel around America or the south of India, as they had planned to do together many years before, she would resent him for the rest of her life, but if he left New York right now without saying anything, silently walking away through that devastated landscape, Adriana would mourn him and feel eternal gratitude toward him. If he vanished into the flames, his son would not grow up thinking that his father was a flake and a deserter but rather a hero. Everyone would remember him with affection instead of resentment. This bizarre conjecture is what roused Moy to make the decision to leave the city and go somewhere far away. Perhaps if he had thought it over for a few more hours, he would have lost the courage to do it, but the urgency with which he had to make up his mind forced his hand. He realized that if the telephone lines came back into operation, sooner or later his cell phone would ring, and Adriana would then know that he had not been fatally injured and was still alive. He took it out of his pocket very deliberately and placed it gently on the ground, on the cement surface of the road. Then he stamped on it repeatedly until it lay in bits. At that moment, he knew that Brandon Moy had died.

A few years later, when I was doing some research on Augusto Pinochet's coup d'état in Chile for my novel *Las manos cortadas*, I found out about a man who, like Moy, had taken advantage of particular circumstances in order to escape. In his case the story had been much more sinister. Pablo Gajardo, a metalworker who lived in Antofagasta, had for several months been trying to find some way of paying off a debt he owed to a loan shark. Neither his parents nor his pregnant wife knew anything about the situation, and he, filled with anxiety over the payment that would soon fall due and the wretchedness of his life, went every afternoon after leaving the factory to spend what little money he had on alcohol to drown his sorrows. He shoplifted and then gambled his ill-gotten gains at cards but ended up losing everything again. Then came the uprising against the Salvador Allende government, which also happened to take place on a September 11. Soldiers arrested hundreds of Chileans in just a few days and killed them. The bodies of a large number of them never reappeared. They were buried in mass graves or thrown into the ocean, they vanished without trace. Pablo Gajardo was not a union member, nor did he have any political ties, but taking advantage of the brutal repression being meted out by the army and the fact that the country had been plunged into chaos, he decided to pass himself off as one of those who had been arrested. He trashed the hellhole in which they lived, emptied the contents of the drawers onto the floor, broke a few worthless objects, and sneaked away. He walked for days until he reached the Peruvian border, and then he settled in Lima. He changed his identity, opened a workshop, and made a fortune. In Chile, everyone thought he was dead. His name appeared among the lists of political exiles, and he was honored as a martyr. In the mid-nineties, when he really did die, one of his Peruvian friends found a cardboard box full of mementos in his house. In it, he had kept a photo of his wife with an inscription on the back, several letters of confession he had never dared to send, and his Chilean identity card. The Peruvian friend wrote to the address on it, and a month later Gajardo's son, who had never gotten to meet his father, replied. Bit by bit, the plot unraveled. The body was not repatriated.

I have often wondered whether I would have the courage to leave behind my home and my loved ones if I were to find myself in circumstances such as those of Pablo Gajardo or if on the contrary, terrified, I would opt for ruin and anguish rather than separating myself from everything that had been my life up to that moment. The story of Brandon Moy is even more exceptional; in his case there had been no clear threat or dangerous situation, just an indeterminate sadness. At forty, or at other less rocky ages, I had felt, as does almost everyone, a desire to completely change my life, to leave Madrid for a distant, faraway city, to find a new job where I could start to learn different things, or to separate myself from my circle of dependable friends, because although I loved them, they shackled me to tarnished, tiresome customs. I never did it, though. At the last minute, I lacked the courage or the determination. I stopped to reflect, as though it were a metaphysical question, on the fact that when we live in a certain way, we stop living in other, different ways, and when we choose a place, we are unable to imagine what might have happened to us in another place. I never knew whether the apprehension or the spinelessness that forced me to remain in Madrid every time an opportunity to leave presented itself would have melted away in circumstances like those that Pablo Gajardo or Brandon Moy experienced. Perhaps each one of us has a crossroads where it's possible for us to peremptorily separate ourselves from everything we possess. Even our memories.

That day, Moy, just like Pablo Gajardo, walked away without stopping. He passed through the streets, trying to escape the clamor and turmoil, and left Manhattan, crossing the Williamsburg Bridge on foot. Without looking back, he marched through Brooklyn, across parks, avenues, and highways, and finally arrived at a secluded place from which, despite the darkness of the night, he could still see the seared New York sky in the distance. Sitting on a slope, he took stock of his belongings— four one-hundred-dollar bills, a laptop, a watch, and a fountain pen. He couldn't use his credit cards, because the financial trail would give him away. He dug a hole with his hands and buried

all his personal documentation right there—
cards, driver's license, and the membership cards
for all the clubs and associations he belonged
to. The only thing he kept from his past life was
a small photo of his son, Brent.

Then he examined his clothes, which were
stained with the dust of the Manhattan air
and, on one side of his jacket, with blood. He
blotted the blood with sandstone to make it
disappear. Then he took off all his clothes
and shook every item. He checked them
meticulously, and when he was sure they had
regained a reasonably elegant appearance, he
got dressed again. He didn't have a mirror to
look at himself, but he thought that as he now
appeared, he would not be taken for a tramp or
a mugger.

He was very hungry and frozen to the
bone, but he fell asleep in the shelter of a small
cave. He recalls that he felt no remorse that
night for what he had just done. His wife and
his child would mourn and be brokenhearted
with grief for a time, but they would soon
end up finding other paths and recovering
their spirits. In a few months, that hellish
night would have been forgotten, and all that
would remain of him would be a melancholy
shadow. Moy closed his eyes and, aghast, could

still see images of men with missing limbs and faces scorched by the fire. Adriana's saturnine eyes, however, did not appear in his nightmares.

The following years of Brandon Moy's life were passionate and intoxicating but would not deserve any literary mention if they had not begun with that feigned, theatrical death. On September 12, while the whole world remained dumbstruck with terror, Moy hitchhiked to Boston, climbing into truck trailers. His head was swarming with thoughts that intertwined and tangled together, thoughts about the disaster, sad memories of the family he had abandoned, and euphoria at the life that, for the first time in so long, lay ahead of him. Images of his son and of naked women mingled in his mind. He felt remorse, and then, an instant later, elation. At the corner of his mouth, a small sore began to develop, a fever blister, and at midmorning he suffered a dizzy spell that forced him to lie down on the shoulder of the highway, dearly hoping someone would pick him up.

One of the drivers who gave him a lift to Boston wanted to talk, affably, about the attacks, but Moy remained silent.

"Ten thousand dead. Or twenty thousand, who knows. Have you ever been to New York?"

"Yes," replied Moy between his teeth, "I was there once a long time ago."

"Did you go up to the top of the towers? They say you get an impressive view of the city."

"I never went up. I don't like heights, I get vertigo."

"You've got to be a real son of a bitch to have done what they did," the man said. "There could be up to thirty thousand dead."

Moy was looking rudely out the car window, ignoring him. Despite the fact that the tragedy had occurred many miles away, there was a gray, leaden air on the sides of the highway, a devastated, arid landscape. The motel and road signs seemed discolored, like signs in places that have had their glory days and then fallen into decrepitude and ruin.

"My wife wanted us to go to New York," continued the man as he drove. "She wanted to go to Tiffany's and have a burger in Times Square. But now, after the massacre, she doesn't feel like it anymore. I, on the other hand, wanna go more than ever. I'm not gonna give those sons of bitches the pleasure of my fear. You know what I think?" he asked, continuing to look straight ahead. "It's time we all go to New York. Tomorrow, this week. All the Americans in New York, everyone at the top of the Empire

State Building. So they get how great this country is."

They stopped to have lunch at a roadside restaurant, and Moy let the man pay for him. His old car, unfashionable clothes, and lack of refinement revealed that he was a humble workingman, but Moy, despite his thousand-dollar suit and his manicured nails, no longer had the option of acting in a dignified manner. Two days earlier he would have been thoroughly ashamed at the situation, but at that moment he felt unperturbed.

"They stole everything," he lied, to justify his poverty. "They took my money, my papers, and my cell phone."

"They left you your briefcase," the man said, pointing at Moy's attaché. He blushed, thinking the man had worked out his lie. He carried on eating in silence, his gaze lost in the window. The man took out his wallet and looked inside it.

"I can lend you twenty dollars. I don't have any more than that."

Moy, with his mouth full, took the bill and stuffed it into the pocket of his pants. He did the math quickly—now he had four hundred and twenty dollars.

It's difficult to imagine how it must feel for such a man to lose everything, even if it is of his own doing. A forty-year-old man who has been affluent his whole life, with a large house full of prized objects, a man who is used to having a glass of whisky before dinner and buying himself new shirts every six months, who has shared his daily life with the same woman for years, and who has devoted most of his free time to rearing his son. Those of you who try to put yourselves in that situation with your own lives will, with good reason, come to imagine that you would miss your books, your clothes, meeting up with friends, the comfort of your bed or sofa, those lazy moments in front of the television, the familiar city streets, and above all, the affection of those you love. Moy himself thought that. In the first few moments, when he was leaving New York with the intention never to return, he thought that he wouldn't be able to live without Adriana's company, without being able to embrace Brent every night when putting him to bed. He thought he wouldn't get used to eating cheap food and drinking low-quality alcohol. He thought he would miss the swimming pool he went to every Monday and the fruit store on his street, where he would stop to talk about baseball with the clerk while picking out apples or strawberries. He thought he would even regret having given up his job, the meetings with clients, and others with the board of directors in which they dealt with the most tiresome matters. He remembered his old saxophone, the collection of jazz records he used to listen to at night when he stayed up working alone, the hammock they hung up in summer on the porch of the Long Island house, and the hourglass he had on his office desk and would sometimes flip over to watch the grains run vertically through its neck. In his ruminations, he was aware of everything important in his life and all those things that were unimportant but had ended up becoming a very personal, categorical form of conduct. What disturbed him most, however, was not any of that but instead a revered social ritual—hygiene. He was less tempted to return to New York to kiss Adriana than to take a bubble bath and put on clean clothes. From the second day, he couldn't stand the humid, sticky sensation of his skin, which adhered clammily to his clothes around his armpits, on his back, and on his feet. He often went into public restrooms, wetted a handkerchief in the sink, and locked himself in a stall in order to strip off his clothes and wash himself, slowly but surely. Even when he was able to take a shower, in the motel where he spent the second night, he continued experiencing the same unpleasant feeling of griminess; his clothes, impregnated with sweat and the filth of life on the street, immediately soiled him again. He took toothpicks from a bar to remove the dirt from under his nails and stole two pairs of socks from a department store, figuring he could squirrel them away without being seen. Often his thoughts wandered to the products in his bathroom in Manhattan: the syrupy gels, the moisturizers, the shampoos, the toothpaste, the colognes. In those moments—and he would later feel remorse as a result—he felt more nostalgia for the warm water faucet than for the affection of his son Brent.

Moy believed during that time, like the romantic poets, that through suffering one could also attain fulfillment. Or, worse still, that only that which is nurtured by torment can be experienced with passion. In truth, he had left New York looking for just that—the razor's edge along which to walk, the unfathomable danger that would turn his life into an adventure. That's why he spent those first few days happy, despite the hardship. In the cold that froze him during the nights as he walked the streets, or in his utter aloneness, without family or friends, he believed he found the essence of life, or at least one of its most poignant roots. And in fact there was some truth in that, because Moy, separated in one fell swoop from everything that had guided his existence until that moment, once again observed the world with the stupefaction and thirst of youth. Just as when we go to another city for a long vacation, we regain the vigor and passion that routine had been insidiously lulling to sleep and we rediscover tastes, pleasures, or predispositions we had forgotten and seem new to us, Moy found over the course of those days the scent of desires, ambitions, and curiosity that had disappeared from his thoughts long ago. He began speculating again, for example about the existence of God, which was a subject that had completely stopped concerning him at the age of sixteen, when he lost his religious faith after the death of one of his grandfathers. He rediscovered the enjoyment to be had in walking down the streets of a place, like Boston, that was new to him, and in staring shamelessly at women, aware that if they responded to the gesture, he could approach them and make a pass.

"In Boston, I learned that life is a contradiction of itself," he told me years later in one of those brotherly conversations we used to have in the bars of Madrid. "I realized that nothing we do makes sense, and that despite that, we still wanna keep doing it. I realized that it's the silliest things that make us the happiest."

Brandon Moy had met the author Paul Auster one day in New York and knew from reading one of his books and from the biographical stories published about him in literary journals that as a young man he had worked as a sailor on an oil tanker and had then spent three years living in Paris, "in a tiny *chambre de bonne* on the sixth floor, barely large enough to hold a bed, a desk, and a chair," as the author said in *The Invention of Solitude*. Despite belonging to a bourgeois family and the fact that he could therefore have had a pleasant life in his own city, had access to comfortable, well-paid jobs, or even asked his father for financial help to spend some time in Europe living the life of a bohemian but without privation, Auster decided to seek out physical asceticism and poverty, to go up against real life. Moy considered that this attitude had shaped not only his character but also his artistic genius. He was convinced that in order to arrive at an understanding of the depths of the human soul, one had to descend into hell, endure hardship, and have one's illusions shattered. He therefore tackled his new situation with a certain sense of joy, as if instead of tolerating a punishment, he were receiving a reward.

In the first few days, while the country was still shuddering from the tragedy of the towers, Moy began to walk the streets of Boston in search of a job that would enable him to pay for food and rent a room until he could get his new life in order. He didn't want to read the newspapers or watch the news on television, and he tried to avoid conversations in the street in which people talked about the catastrophe of the towers; his spirit was not yet ready to learn anything about his own death. At mid afternoon on the third day, he saw a sign in the window of a downtown coffee shop, advertizing a position for a waiter. He dusted off his clothes, ran his fingers through his hair, sniffed his armpits, which he had just washed in the restroom of another establishment, and went in to put himself forward for the job. The manager examined his appearance with suspicion; Moy was neither dressed in the way that candidates for the post usually were, nor was he of the usual age, and he asked him several questions about his experience. Moy lied with a naturalness that surprised even himself. He told a sad story—desertion by his wife and a mugging—and made up previous jobs in restaurants in Pittsburgh and New York. Then the manager spoke to him about the Twin Towers and the curse of Islamic fundamentalism. Moy went along with him, struck up a rapport, and got the job, in which his salary would consist only of the tips he collected.

"What's your name?" the man asked.

Moy turned pale. Although he was aware that in order to return to life he would have to completely change his identity, he had not planned anything in that regard. He stuttered and delved into his memory for a face to which he could tie his future.

"Albert," he replied hastily. "Albert."

"Albert what? I need to know who I'm hiring."

Moy stuttered again. He knew he couldn't call himself Albert Fergus, because that thread, in time, could easily become a rope.

"Tracy," he said, in a flash of revelation. "Like Spencer Tracy."

The manager treated him to a hot cup of coffee and a piece of cake, which Moy tried to eat while at the same time disguising his hunger. That day, when he left there, he had to steal. He needed to get a thorough wash and buy some casual clothes, some jeans, a T-shirt, and a warm sweater, in order to present himself the following day at the coffee shop. He walked until he reached a quiet neighborhood, and on one of those silent streets lined with gardens and low-rise houses one finds in Boston, he waited for a victim. He had never committed a crime in his life, other than traffic offences and the odd small-scale tax dodge, but he knew he had to do it. It was not only necessary in order to get his new life on track financially but also formed one more link in the chain of experience he wanted to possess. He was certain that Fergus had stolen something at some point, and it was even possible that he had been arrested and spent a while in prison. These thoughts, which appeared abruptly in his head, paralyzed him. The idea of being arrested and returning to New York in disgrace for having committed a crime, which would make him lose the esteem of his son as well as his own dignity, frightened him. He suddenly realized that what he was doing was absolute madness. He could be in his house in Manhattan, comfortably sharing dinner with Adriana and watching the news about the havoc caused by the terrorists, but instead he was on a dark street in Boston, lying in wait to mug an unsuspecting passerby. He felt a veil being lifted from his eyes and the entanglement of his existential theories waning. He started walking away, and when he reached a busier area, he looked for a telephone booth from which he could call Adriana to tell her he was still alive and that he would go home immediately. He spent a few minutes concocting a plausible story to explain his disappearance to her. In the end he decided he would use the excuse of amnesia—he couldn't remember anything, he didn't know how he had survived the attack or how he had ended up in Boston. Until a few moments ago, he didn't even remember who he was, his name, or where he lived; he had spent the last few days living like a beggar, but now, all of a sudden, his memories had come back. He would tell Adriana that he loved her and that he was longing to get back to her. In a faltering voice, he would ask about Brent and would then effortlessly burst into tears so that she would be in no doubt that what he was saying was true. Although, in reality, nobody would ever believe it wasn't; who would ever think that Moy had faked his own death in order to walk away from his peaceful, comfortable life? Who would ever suspect that he would give up his son and his wealth in order to experience the ordeal of being a wayfarer? It was such nonsense and so irrational that no levelheaded person would be able to make any sense of it.

Moy remembers that he even got as far as taking a coin out of his pocket and walking up to the telephone booth. At that moment, everything could have come to an end, but as he picked up the receiver, he saw an older woman on the other side of the road, walking toward him very slowly, and limping. She carried a large bag awkwardly under her arm. Moy waited a few seconds until the woman's position was even with his, and then, without further thought, his nerves suffocating him, he stepped out of the booth, grabbed one end of the bag, and ran, taking huge strides until he was out of sight. He didn't hear the woman shout or sense people running after him, but he still did not stop. Only when he arrived at a deserted spot that must have been on the outskirts of Boston did he sit on the ground to rest, gasping for breath. He was no longer thinking about Adriana or Brent but rather about the euphoria he'd felt while escaping, about the feverish excitement that had coursed through his body when he'd snatched the bag from the woman's arms. He could still feel the current of adrenaline in his muscles, a sort of tingling sensation. His legs were trembling, and his lips were stiff and dry. After a few moments he realized he still had the coin he had been going to use in the telephone booth to call Adriana, in his left hand, which was balled into a fist. He never got rid of it. Like millionaires who keep their first dollar, Moy saved that coin so that it would bring him luck, although for a long time he was unsure what his luck might entail.

The bag contained a makeup pouch, a pair of prescription glasses, a missal, a cell phone, some papers, and nearly two hundred dollars, hidden in an inside pocket. Moy kept the money and threw the rest of the contents into a dumpster, making sure the bag was well buried among the trash so that nobody would find it by chance. Then he looked for a quiet, well-lit place and started to think through what he needed. He had to buy some jeans, some sort of garment to keep him warm, and at least two shirts, so that he could alternate them. Underwear, which was out of sight, could wait until times were better. On the other hand, he should get a hold of several pairs of socks without delay, because he found having dirty feet particularly intolerable. The shoes he was wearing were too fancy and only went well with a suit or elegant clothing, but he could manage with them until he saved enough to buy some sneakers.

In addition to the clothes, there were other, equally pressing needs. First of all, he had to find a cheap room that would provide him with a permanent place to sleep. Hotels and motels were too costly, so he had to look in the classifieds for a private house in which rooms were being let short term. And if he made himself look more presentable, he was sure that he could convince someone to trust him for a few days until he got together a month's rent with his tips. It was not necessary to consider food expenses; during this time of austerity and abstinence, he could survive on what he ate at the coffee shop and even keep the leftovers as a supply in the event of there being even harder times ahead.

But the biggest outlay Moy would have to make over the following days had nothing to do with household expenses, it was instead of a more murky, thorny nature—he had to obtain false identity documents as soon as possible in the name of Albert Tracy. Along with fictitious information from police movies and newspaper articles about fraud and identity theft, Moy had come across the real stories of those criminal networks through some of the law firm's clients, who on several occasions had been conned with false identity documents. He didn't fully understand the process of falsification, nor did he know the cost, but he knew that he could easily get in touch online with small-time crooks who made passports, driver's licenses, and Social Security cards for cheap. That same afternoon, he went into an internet café in downtown Boston and searched for a clue that would enable him to reach those networks, or their perimeters. Surfing page by page, carefully scanning forums and chat rooms, he obtained two email addresses he could write to. He opened a Hotmail account with false personal details, and from it he wrote to those addresses, asking for information as though it were a job application or an administrative request.

On leaving the internet café, he stole one of the newspapers that was on the counter for clients to read and looked for room rentals in the classifieds. Then, by chance, something happened that changed the course of events. Moy saw the personal ads, which came after the real estate section, and started to glance through them. Almost all of them were from gay men or men seeking relationships with women, but there were three written by older women hoping to find gentlemen with whom they could share their lives, or with whom they could at least share some of its pleasures. Moy read them carefully several times and chose one he found suggestive. A fifty-year-old woman who claimed she was in perfect shape, with a youthful body, was searching for an ardent man—that's the word she used, *ardent*—who could assuage the sorrows of growing older. Moy, who had never felt any particular attraction toward older women, found himself aroused by this ad, which was so frank and so direct and completely avoided getting sidetracked with ambiguities or taking refuge in false hopes. He felt compassion for this woman and imagined himself in her bed as if instead of being a lover, he were a philanthropist, bringing her pleasure to assuage her sorrow and showing her erotic secrets to help her forget the adversities of the world. He called her immediately and was talking to her for almost an hour. Moy lied about everything—he told her that he had just gone through a divorce, that he had moved from Pittsburgh a few days ago and wanted to start a new life in Boston, far away from the tribulations of the past. They discovered that they were both fans of Ella Fitzgerald and both liked salads and Enid Blyton novels, which Moy had read as a child. Both of them enjoyed driving and getting up early. She was called Daisy, and she wanted to learn how to dance and how to plant flowers in her garden, but the idea of doing those things alone did not appeal to her. She was shy, and when Moy began to get more intimate, making insinuations about sexual matters, she fell silent, breathing uneasily on the other end of the line. He had the notion that Daisy might invite him to go and sleep over at her house that very night but immediately realized that given how he looked, unwashed and badly dressed, it would have been a disaster. They arranged a date for the following day at a café downtown, near the place where he was going to start work, and they said goodbye with a courtesy that was almost trite, old-fashioned, and made Moy imagine that Daisy was one of those women who felt flattered when given flowers or when someone pulled out the chair in a restaurant so that they could sit down.

In a discount store near the internet café, he bought the clothes he needed. Then he went into a dry cleaner's and asked the clerk to clean his suit using the cheapest method available, even if it didn't look immaculate afterward. He begged her with more lies to have it ready for him the next day without adding an extra charge for the rush, and the assistant, either because she was touched or irritated, promised to do it. Finally, when it was dark, Moy looked for a hotel where he could sleep. He spent seventy dollars on a comfortable room. Before going to bed, he had a very hot bath and watched how the grime accumulated over the last several days sloughed off his body; it was like a baptism that not only stripped away the dirt and the encrusted sweat but also the iniquity of his escape.

Brandon Moy had an inscrutable, complicated personality, and there was a moment when I began to think he was crazy and that all the things he had told me were delusions or figments of his imagination. Perhaps before the attack on the towers, in his routine life in New York, he had been an ordinary man who thought in a logical, orderly manner. On the other hand, when I spoke to him, his speech was neither methodical nor coherent. The links between his memories and the facts kept changing as his mood altered or as some coincidental association of ideas derailed his memory's train of thought. The first time he spoke to me about that day in Boston, that seventy-dollar hotel where he had washed away the filth and his sins in boiling water, he explained to me that when he went to bed afterward, he felt an extraordinary happiness, like that which one only experiences during childhood. He'd thought that at last he was living the life he was meant to live and that those trials—the dirt, the poverty, and not even having a book to read before going to sleep— were simply manifestations of the fulfillment he was pursuing. He had no assurances about what would happen to him the following day, and that fact, which for so long had seemed threatening to him, now struck him as fortunate. Several months later, however, he described those days following September 11 to me again, but this time he didn't mention that they had been happy and fruitful, he didn't speak to me of the euphoria or the joy he had felt, that night in the mid-range hotel in Boston, when thinking about the freedom he would have from that moment on to sleep with strangers or experience extreme emotions. On the contrary, he assured me that he had been awake the whole night, crying with a panicky, stifling unease, and that several times he had been on the point of calling Adriana from his room and asking her to pick him up. He admitted to me that he had begun to think about suicide, about buying sleeping pills, or jumping off the top of a building. He had even gone so far as leaning out of the hotel window in the middle of the night, but the room was on the second floor, and the grotesque scene of an unsuccessful suicide frightened him. The two versions of the story, the sublime and the dramatic, that of joy and that of desperation, were full of specific details, of tangible minutiae that gave the impression the memories were genuine. The scissors he had asked for in reception to cut his nails, the outdated pattern on the wallpaper, the flimsiness of the pillows, the bluish color of the bedside lamps, the warnings penciled in the margins of the Bible in the drawer of the nightstand, and the shouting coming from one of the neighboring rooms gave a very real feel to his description of his moods, from joyful to depressed, and he passed them off as true. It's possible that that night, Moy felt great vulnerability and wonderful hope at the same time, as if they were two sides of the same coin. There is no doubt that he felt lonely, and exposed, and terrified by the future, but at the same time, he must have imagined, as he had done outside that restaurant in New York after talking to Albert Fergus, extraordinary thrills ahead of him—naked women, success, adventures, and superhuman experiences. Over time, troubled by the contradiction, he would have dissociated these antagonistic images to the point of turning that one night into two different nights, one pleasurable and the other dismal. It's what we all almost always do, for example, when remembering our adolescent years.

Whether he slept deeply or spent the night awake, Moy got up on time the following morning, washed again, put on his new clothes, and left the hotel. Before going to the coffee shop at the time he had agreed on with the owner, he called various people who were advertising rooms for rent in the Boston Globe and arranged to meet with two of them that afternoon. Then he found an internet café and checked his email—nobody had replied to him. At midmorning, right on time, he went into the coffee shop and started work. There weren't many customers, but he managed to collect almost seventy dollars in tips. He realized with surprise that all trades have their problems and stumbling blocks. Despite his inexperience with all the trays and orders, he took great pains to make a good job of the service and quickly learn the necessary tricks. He was friendly and hardworking. He obeyed everything the manager told him and tried to pay attention to his frowns and gesticulations in order to work out in advance the opinion he would have of him. At the end of the day, at shift handover, he ate the leftovers of cakes and sandwiches and then said goodbye, exhausted by all the effort. The manager congratulated him.

When he checked his email account again, he had received a reply from one of the forgers he had written to the day before. Using cautious language full of tacit statements, the forger explained that what he was looking for could be obtained in ten days without any difficulties or risk, but the price was five thousand dollars, half of which had to be paid in advance. He offered him the opportunity to handle it all by mail, as if it were a regular administrative procedure, or to have a face-to-face appointment if he preferred. In either case, he only needed to hand over some passport-size photos, as well, of course, as the money.

Moy felt reassured that there had been a reply; it was the final confirmation that turning into someone else was a bureaucratically simple process. The price, however, alarmed him. A few days before, in New York, he would have thought it was cheap—just five thousand dollars, the price of one month's rent for an apartment like the one he had, to turn into a different man, a person whose past is a blank or transparent slate on which everything can be rewritten. He thought, pompously, that a new life cost less than most cars, than a trip to Europe, or even a designer coat. At that moment, however, five thousand dollars was an unattainable fortune for him. There was almost one hundred times that amount in his checking account and his securities portfolio, but only Brandon Moy could access it, and he had died in September in the attack on the Twin Towers.

He went to his date with Daisy wearing the suit he had just freshened up and with the rest of his clothes in a large bag. He bought her a rose, which as he had predicted, delighted her. Daisy was a slightly built woman. Despite her age she was still pretty, but the heavy makeup she wore, combining shades of fuchsia and dark blue, gave her appearance a kitsch, unsophisticated look. Her hair was badly dyed, and she had long nails decorated with arabesques.

Moy realized immediately that if he acted shrewdly, he could get whatever he wanted from her. He told her the story of his divorce again and, feigning embarrassment at the disgrace, admitted that he was broke.

"I'm not a good catch," he said without looking at her, as though the shame were smothering him.

Daisy tried to console him. They talked about movies, the life of Ella Fitzgerald, and the trips one can take from Boston—Green Mountain National Forest, Cape Cod, the New England coast, and further afield, Montreal and the southern region of Canada. Moy enthusiastically explained to her that he thoroughly enjoyed traveling but that he hadn't gotten the chance to do it with his wife. When Daisy suggested they go to her house for dinner, bragging about what an excellent cook she was, Moy was certain this woman could be the lifeline he needed.

It had never been his wish to hurt her or take advantage of her kindness, although the line between that and deception was very fine. Moy found sleeping with Daisy pleasurable, so he never came to think of his behavior as being like that of a gigolo, or that the financial benefit he got out of it was tainted by disloyalty. Moved to pity by the misfortunes he told her about, Daisy suggested straightaway that he come to live at her place, and she helped him to get his life in order. She gave him some clothes that had belonged to her dead husband, in large sizes and loud colors, and she lent him the five thousand dollars he asked her for under the pretext of paying off an old debt.

"Do you believe in God?" she asked him on one of their first days together, as they finished dinner. "In the true God, I mean."

Moy looked at her affectionately. That trusting naïveté made her seem so fragile and airy.

"Which is the true God?"

She blushed and looked away. Her lips were painted with glossy, jarring lipstick that the drumming of her fingertips on her mouth had also transferred to her cheeks.

"The true God," she repeated without looking at him. "The God of men who don't kill."

Moy had tried to steer clear of the news about the terrorist attacks, to avoid his own pangs of conscience, but it was impossible to do so completely. He didn't read the newspapers, except for the classifieds, and he tried to keep away from the television, but the customers at the coffee shop, the preachers who sounded off at the top of their voices in the streets, and the huge posters everywhere bearing apocalyptic messages prevented him from being able to forget the New York tragedy. He knew George W. Bush's administration was searching for the al-Qaeda terrorists who had survived and that the entire country was on the hunt for Islamic fundamentalists. The men who believed in a God that was not the true one.

"I don't know whether I believe in God," replied Moy sweetly, "but if I did believe in one, it would definitely be the true one."

Moy had not been able to elude the memories of his colleagues at Robertson & Millyander or prevent himself from conjuring up scenes of their deaths. He wondered if they had jumped out one of the windows, as he had seen many of those who were trapped in the building do, if they'd been burnt to a crisp by the flames, or if they were sucked down, still alive, with the tower as it collapsed. He thought about Bob, who had joined the team a month ago and was still awestruck at working in the World Trade Center; every morning, when he got to the office, he would be glued to the windows, gazing at the high-rise skyline as he drank his cup of coffee. He wasn't yet thirty, and he dreamed of climbing even higher. Perhaps he had seen the planes arrive. Moy also remembered Nancy, his secretary, with whom he had shared dilemmas and the daily hustle and bustle for seven years. And Martin, who had just been diagnosed with a disease from which he would now never recover.

But what tormented Moy more than all the memories of other people and the phantasmagoric imaginings with which he concocted their deaths was imagining how he would have acted if he had been in the building, in his office on the ninety-sixth floor of the North Tower, like on any other morning. He tried to envisage the horror of that image, as though it were a penance. Would he have started to weep and have hysterical convulsions as he had done when he had been stuck in an elevator as a child? Would he have tried to escape, casting dignity aside and pushing the weak to the ground in order to step over them? Would he have felt panic, or serenity, on sensing his impending death? Basically, he told himself mockingly, none of the fascinating adventures that Albert Fergus had experienced or that he himself was hoping to have from this moment on were comparable in size, depth, or merit to that of being trapped in a building that had been ripped open by the impact of a plane and having an inexorable and brutal sense of the fading pulse of time and the fragility of the things that are closest to you. What kinds of feelings grip the heart of a man who has thrown himself out of one of the top floors of a hundred-story building? What does he think during those ten seconds it takes before he smashes into the ground? What does he think in the final second, when he can see the outline of his shadow on the sidewalk? Does he remember someone, imagine death, or, as in hallucinations, see spiraling, intertwining colors swirling in the irises of his eyes? Nobody can know. It is an experience that cannot be recounted.

Brandon Moy lived with Daisy for five months, but during that time, he was frequently unfaithful to her. He suddenly discovered that if he was alert and willing to following the rules of sexual courtship, it was very easy to bed a woman. He was an attractive man with an athletic body, blue eyes, and a dazzling smile that lit up his face, even when it had a wistful tinge. Some of the coffee shop customers, especially women who were there on their own, would sit watching him, intrigued, and order another drink to draw out the time. Moy learned quickly how to discern their gestures and interpret their intentions. If he was attracted to one of these women, he would return her glances furtively, so that she wouldn't think he was brazen or lecherous. He would go out of his way to treat her well and would take great pains with the service. He always left it to her to start the conversation. Then everything was simple; Moy knew that after a certain point, boldness paid off, it livened up the game and speeded desire. They would arrange a date, choose a place to go, and sleep together. Moy, who had always been very fastidious with regard to matters of the flesh, began little by little to grow intoxicated by that erotic whirlwind and after several weeks was obsessed with having sex with all the women he liked, as if he wanted to suddenly make up for the period of abstinence during his marriage. He paid attention to older ladies, like Daisy, and girls that were little more than teenagers. With each age, he found a sensual uniqueness and an aesthetic sensibility; Daisy's delicate flesh, her stretch-marked thighs, and flaccid breasts belonged to a different zoological species than that of a girl of twenty, in his opinion. The lovemaking skills of one woman as opposed to the other—obscenity as opposed to inexperience—were like different genres of literature that could not be compared, like chivalric romances and lyrical poetry.

He regretted having spent so many years unconcernedly committed to the sexual ceremonies that he and Adriana repeated out of habit and that, although pleasant, didn't make him lose himself or forget about death. Orgasms now, in Boston, shocked him—in an instant all his thoughts were erased and the only thing he could see was a brilliant expanse that blinded him. Then he would collapse, exhausted, on the bed, and it would take some time to regain consciousness. He experienced such extraordinary happiness that he couldn't let a single day go by without seeking it out. If he didn't meet anyone at the coffee shop, he called one of the last few women he had been with, and if that move didn't work either, he would turn to the classifieds in the *Boston Globe*, where it was always easy to find promising victims. He could not yet afford to visit prostitutes, but on those days when he ended up on his own or unsatisfied, the idea of doing so tempted him.

He broke up with Daisy, because he wasn't capable of pleasing her sexually without neglecting those other desires that controlled him with increasing urgency. Sometimes she would show up unexpectedly at the coffee shop to pick him up, ruining the date he had planned. On other occasions, when Moy returned home at night after having been with another woman, Daisy would try to arouse him with flattery and embraces, and he, his vigor unable to withstand so many onslaughts, would have to feign some ailment in order to excuse himself. In the end, he started to look for a place he could move to, so as not to find himself under the same conjugal obligations with Daisy that he had wanted to break away from with Adriana. The separation was not dramatic. She cried but made him promise that he would continue visiting her. Moy, who at that time still owed her a thousand dollars of the loan she had given him to pay for the Albert Tracy ID, more than kept his promise, since on days when he didn't manage to make a successful pass at any other woman, he would call Daisy and spend the night with her.

During those first few months of his new life, Brandon Moy only allowed himself irrational chaos in this one area. In all other matters, he strove to once again maintain a suitable balance—he followed a strict schedule, behaved professionally at the coffee shop, kept a stringent check on his income and expenses, and in short did not do anything that could compromise him or cloud his judgment. One day, by chance, he found himself in front of the window of a music shop, and knowing full well that he did not have money to spend on luxuries, he went in to ask the price of the saxophones. Over the course of those several weeks, he also wanted to sign up for a writing course and a French course, but he couldn't pay for either of them. Women became the only desire he could access free of charge and in excess.

He would jot down his future plans in a notebook. He made a list of professions that appealed to him and included some that were ridiculous and he could never do: jeweler, taxi driver, astronaut, landscape architect, photographer, riding instructor (although he had never ridden a horse), topographer, singer, ship's captain, and tailor. He also considered the possibility of continuing to practice as a lawyer, since despite the irritating tedium he had endured for years at Robertson & Millyander drafting contracts for bankers and financial agencies, he was aware that there were other legal activities that better suited his temperament. Moy had always voted for the Democratic Party and had even worked as a volunteer in Al Gore's electoral campaign a few months earlier. He was interested in the areas of civil rights, legal aid for detainees without means, and social work, in which he knew some participating activist organizations that desperately needed experienced lawyers.

In the same notebook, which he still had when I met him, he also made a list of things he dreamed of and challenges he'd set for himself—as well as learning French and taking up the saxophone again, he wanted to go up in a hot air balloon, go scuba diving, study anthropology, travel to Europe, attend a bullfight, get involved in car racing, have a homosexual experience, take hallucinogenic drugs, sail on the high seas, take piano lessons, do fencing, and learn how to dance the tango, the samba, and the foxtrot, as Daisy had wanted him to do. With the exception of two of them—the anthropology, which he only pursued by chaotically reading a few books, and the fencing—he fulfilled all his aims. But in so doing, he didn't find the satisfaction he had hoped for.

He didn't put literature down either on the list of professions in which he wanted to work or among the dreams he wanted to realize, but he did devote several pages to it in his notebook, making a disorganized record of a range of books he had to read and scribbling some notes with plot lines for stories he intended to write. Since his college days, when he had written a set of science fiction stories with Fergus that naïvely examined alien life, the mechanisms of human evolution, and technical development, reveling (he more than Fergus) in descriptions of fantastical machines and spacecraft with almost magical capabilities, Moy hadn't written anything other than legal reports and financial contracts. Despite the fact that it was an activity he thoroughly enjoyed, he had never subsequently missed it with any great longing, unlike his other, more burning passions such as the saxophone or mountain climbing. During those days in Boston, however, he felt the need to scrawl disjointed ideas and personal reflections in his notebook, which enabled him to let off steam. Everything he couldn't tell anybody—that he had abandoned a woman he loved, that he felt a terrible sense of guilt over the imagined unhappiness of his son, that life was a vortex from which there was no escape—he wrote in the notebook. He came up with several ideas and began to draft some stories. He had never been interested in poetry, and he didn't have any background in the lyrical arts. He had never written verse. It was therefore quite unforeseeable that he would end up composing one of the most original and brilliant poetry collections of the early twenty-first century and becoming a cult author. Just like most important life events, like his escape from New York, it happened by chance.

One day in Quincy Market he met an Australian girl who was studying literature at Harvard University. He accompanied her to the dorm room she shared with two other students and slept with her. Afterward, they stayed in bed talking, both of them naked, and the girl passionately explained to him who her favorite authors were. There were a few that Moy had never heard of or at least only knew of vaguely. The girl, who undoubtedly felt for him the kind of existential admiration that older men elicit at a certain age, saw the chance to grow in his estimation, and so, feigning shock at Moy's ignorance, she got out of bed, rummaged through the piles of books that were stacked on the floor of the room, and handed him a bilingual volume of the poetry of Rainer Maria Rilke, about whom Moy knew absolutely nothing. He, flattered and amused by that unexpected burst of literary training, flicked through it in front of her and then threw himself back into the conversation. Later on, when he left the apartment, he took the book out of courtesy. He had no definite intention of reading it, but when he got home, he sat in an armchair, piqued by curiosity, opened it near the beginning, and began to study it with more enthusiasm than he had expected.

They began to meet up regularly, and the poetry always came after the impropriety. The Australian girl introduced him to the works of

Kokoschka, D'Annunzio, Henri Michaux, and Sylvia Plath, whose names were completely unknown to him up until that moment. In this way, little by little, they created a bond, or a fellowship, with each other, and one day, sullen and saddened by the mood swings he just could not bring under control, Moy dared to tell her his story. She listened to him attentively for two hours. Then she got out of bed, dug around again among the clutter of books, and presented him with a brief work by Constantine Cavafy, opened to one page. Moy, still undressed, lying on the Australian girl's bed in the dark, read the poem "The City" aloud in a quiet voice, and as though it had been written just for him almost a century earlier, it tore his heart to pieces and made him weep until sorrow left him exhausted.

You said:"I'll go to another country, go to another shore,
find another city better than this one.
Whatever I try to do is fated to turn out wrong
and my heart lies buried as though it were
something dead.
How long can I let my mind moulder in this place?
Wherever I turn, wherever I happen to look,
I see the black ruins of my life, here,
where I've spent so many years, wasted them,
destroyed them totally."

You won't find a new country, won't find another shore.
This city will always pursue you. You will walk
the same streets, grow old in the same neighborhoods,
will turn gray in these same houses.
You will always end up in this city. Don't hope for
   things elsewhere:
there is no ship for you, there is no road.
As you've wasted your life here, in this small corner,
you've destroyed it everywhere else in the world.

Up until that moment, Brandon Moy had considered that perhaps novels and poetry were first and foremost highbrow entertainment, a sophisticated, refined hobby, but that day, upon seeing the essence of his life story encapsulated in sixteen lines by a Greek poet who had died long before he was born, he realized that literature possessed a dark, syrupy essence that served as a skeletal support for living. He was frightened by the prophecy, as if instead of having read a poem, he had heard voices in a séance or had witnessed the appearance of a specter in the middle of the night. He felt that perhaps everything that was foretold there would come to pass, and that then he would have to regret abandoning Adriana and Brent in vain. That feeling of terror, which he had never before felt as a result of reading something, seized him completely. The next day, at his house, he continued reading the poems from the moment he woke up, and was so enthralled by them that, for the first time, he arrived at the coffee shop late. On leaving work he called the Australian girl, and they met up again to talk about literature. After Daisy, she was the woman in Boston with whom he had the longest relationship. She was fascinated by having a mature, experienced lover, and he received poetry lessons between sex sessions and borrowed books from her that he devoured with almost erotic fervor. He didn't find any other omens in them, but he was learning how to find his way through labyrinths. It was still a long time before he started writing his own poetry, and when he did so, he discovered, disheartened, that the intricacies of his own words brought him less relief than those written by others that he endeavored to read.

His collection of poems, titled *The City*, like the poem by Cavafy, was translated into Spanish by a Mexican publisher in 2008. That's the version I read, since I have a very limited mastery of English, and although I don't have much capacity for judgment when it comes to poetry, through its pages I understood the bleakness that Moy had felt during his journey from New York to the end of the world and, at the same time, the joy harboring within that grief. In order to understand the true basis of his thoughts, I found (as has happened to me also with some other writer friends) that painstakingly poring over his poems was more useful than the confessional conversations we had. Friendship and alcohol hone frankness, but writing goes further, reaching the innermost recesses of what a person knows and can tell.

Brandon Moy's romantic adventures steered his life for some time. Among all the women he met over the course of those months, the most important one for his future was Laureen, who was married to a somewhat elderly and influential Italian diplomat. It was she who, like in the myth of Pygmalion, completed the task the Australian student had begun, educating him in certain artistic disciplines and acquainting him with the cultural circles of the city. She introduced him to painters, musicians, and writers and later, when Moy had left Boston, put him in touch with Richard Palfrey, the Los Angeles editor who published his poetry collection. He always showed devotion to this woman and met up with her again years later in Europe. He visited her in Rome, where she had retired with her diplomat husband, and they journeyed together around several Italian cities.

After he had left Daisy and was living alone in a rented room in Back Bay, Moy met a wealthy woman through the classifieds in the *Boston Globe* who became infatuated with him and started to flaunt him at high society get-togethers, different charitable events she attended, and meetings of Republican Party political committees. This lady, who had just gone through a period of depression following the death of her only child and who took half a cupful of painkillers, hypnotics, and sedatives everyday to balance her mood, welcomed him into her home, just like Daisy, and offered him a job as her personal assistant. Moy had immediately understood that one of the great advantages of his new situation was being able to invent a past at his convenience, adorning it with amazing achievements or making it suit the situations that arose as required, and he told her a farfetched story in which there were deaths, betrayals, rejections in love, and corporate conspiracies. According to this tale, Moy had for two years been the personal assistant to the president of a major telecommunications company, the name of which he did not divulge, in order to maintain confidentiality. He kept this man's private accounts, managed non-transparent companies in tax havens, and generally dealt with all those matters that required some kind of discreet legal advice. After a time, he had started a relationship with the boss's wife, who shamelessly flirted with him. They saw each other secretly in hotels or in the house when her husband was away. On one of those occasions, he left a scarf in the bedroom, and his boss found out about the affair. He had been forced to bolt from the city without any of his belongings but had taken with him some compromising documents that protected him from the wrath of the jealous husband. For a few months he had been counting on his lady friend joining him in Boston, but then soon realized he didn't really love her. He was working as a waiter in a coffee shop while he put his life back together.

The melodramatic stories with which Brandon Moy introduced himself to the people he met after escaping from New York, like this one about the corrupt, jealous businessman, which sounded like something out of a mediocre screenplay, enabled him to indulge in risky, exciting exploits without the danger of actually going through them. As writers often do to fulfill fantasies that are out of reach, Moy recreated in his imagination the extraordinary events to which he was drawn. He told people about astonishing happenings, and even he came to believe that his existence was less humdrum than in the past.

The tasks this wealthy lady entrusted to him involved accompanying her to social events, writing letters for her by hand, helping her when she went shopping, and warming her bed at night. For a time, Moy remained faithful to her, but not because he wanted to, rather because it was impossible to escape her watchfulness. And so for him, seduction not only became a sexual challenge but also a test of his cunning, since finding daring ways of outsmarting her surveillance was something he found provocative and pleasurable. If one day, during the course of an evening, an ugly, repulsive female looked lasciviously at him, Moy, who would never have been interested in her under other circumstances, felt frustrated at not being able to approach her and make a pass. Gradually, however, he started creating schemes and tricks to accomplish his desire. On one occasion, he slept with one of the woman's friends, having been sent to her house in order to return a powder compact she had lent to his lover the night before. At one of the hotels where they would stay on their weekend trips, he took advantage of the woman's deep sleep to go to the bedroom of an employee with whom he had flirted during dinner. And he insisted on being the one to take the woman's hound dog for its nightly walk, in order to have some short-lived fling nearby.

Those days were accompanied by the presence of a new temptation, one he ended up satisfying. Since the woman was very rich and he had access to her secret accounts, which were difficult to trace, he planned to embezzle the funds and escape to Mexico, following in the distant steps of Albert Fergus. According to his testimony—which might not be honest—the risk of committing the crime was more attractive to him than the money he would be able to amass. But he was afraid that if caught by the federal police, his previous life might be discovered and he would be exposed in front of his wife and son, which for him, at this stage of his adventure, was the very idea of hell. He therefore decided to be cautious and only extract small amounts that would lessen the danger. He put to use all the knowledge he had gathered over the years at Robertson & Millyander, and despite his wise restraint, he managed to accumulate thirty-five thousand dollars in a few months, which according to his calculations would allow him to live easily for a year in Mexico, devoting himself to literature, diving, and the study, paradoxically, of *lucha libre* and ballroom dancing.

Sometimes, when he walked through downtown Boston, he liked to visit the coffee shop where he had worked, to have a drink and say hello to his coworkers. It was there that he heard about the story of Feliciano Jaramillo, the brother of the Columbian girl who had been hired to replace him. Jaramillo had been in the United States for five years. He'd crossed the border illegally after traveling across Central America hidden in cargo trucks and had had several off-the-books jobs before arriving in Boston. In spite of the money he'd sent to his sister for her flight to join him there and the sums he sent home every month to his family in Taganga, a small fishing village in the Caribbean, he'd managed to save a small amount, with which he hoped to one day be able to afford rent to open up a business. The opportunity was precipitately offered to him by the manager of the apartment block where he lived, who told him about a cooperative of immigrants who were trying to raise enough money to lease and refurbish a motel on the outskirts of the city. They were looking for partners who, as well as contributing capital, would be willing to then work in the establishment. Jaramillo, pleased with his good luck, went to see the motel, unearthed two wads of bills, and trustingly handed them to the manager, who in return gave him a document signed by the supposed president of the cooperative. The weeks went by, and when Jaramillo demanded news about the business, the manager assured him that they still needed to top up the capital and that it was therefore not yet possible to sign off on the lease. Three months later Jaramillo, by then suspicious, asked to see the president of the cooperative. The manager took him to see a scruffy, half-drunk man who gave him incoherent explanations and promised him that he could be working in the motel in less than sixty days. That time passed without any progress, and Jaramillo, tormented by doubts, showed up at the manager's office to demand his money back. There was a heated argument. The manager told him that he was only an impartial middleman and couldn't give him any information about his investment. He suggested that he take the document to the police in order to seek justice. Then, when Jaramillo began to roar with fury and broke one of the objects on his desk, he threw him out of the office and gave him forty-eight hours to vacate the room in which he lived. Jaramillo, who didn't have United States residency papers and therefore couldn't turn to the law, suddenly found himself broke and evicted from his home. The adversities, however, did not end there. A few days later, the immigration police went and located him at the repair shop where he worked and arrested him. He was in prison awaiting deportation.

Angelita, his sister, couldn't stop crying as she told Moy the story. She showed him the worthless document and went with him to the motel the next day, where they confirmed the business had never been for sale and that as a result, the deal with the cooperative had been nothing more than a scam. Moy, who felt sorry for Angelita and for Feliciano's misfortune, saw for the first time the opportunity to do something memorable with his new life. He explained to the girl that he was a lawyer and would like to try to defend her brother, so that even if he couldn't recover the money, he would avoid being deported. Angelita, who was twenty years old, yielded to his kindness and fell in love with him. She was the first great passion in Albert Tracy's life.

When he first started meeting with Feliciano Jaramillo in prison and studying his case, Moy, who had been somewhat naïve, came to understand the social burdens that determine a person's destiny. One year before, in September 2001, he had possessed absolutely nothing. A suit, a pair of shoes, and four hundred dollars. A few months later he had accumulated a modest sum (even if it was obtained by stealing from someone who had more than he did), was wearing expensive clothes, going to fashionable restaurants, and had access to some of Boston's most elegant venues. Jaramillo, on the other hand, would never have anything close to that. If he restarted his life one hundred times over, he would fail a hundred times. Perhaps he might achieve a certain level of well-being—a comfortable house, a plate of hot food everyday, an obliging wife—but he would never be capable of breaking through to prosperity. He had dark skin and indigenous features. He knew how to read, but hardly ever understood the words he was reading. He treated people with a respect that wasn't courtesy but rather obsequiousness.

This discovery of the afflictions of the world transformed Moy's conscience. He became a romantic idealist who imagined poverty to be a kind of spiritual salvation that had to be preserved. During the process of Jaramillo's defense, while he compiled information and researched the legal aid and protection systems for the most humble social classes, a feeling of revolutionary morality began to take shape in him. Suddenly he was aware of the atrocities that were committed with impunity against those who were defenseless, and he journeyed through the dark vaults in which justice was dealt out. Like Saul in Damascus, he was astonished by the evils of humanity in such close proximity, and he decided to devote his life to helping others.

"Don Quixote left his little village to protect the weak and right the twisted ways of the world," I said to him on one occasion. "He left to have adventures and an admirable life."

During that fleeting time of ideological change, Moy began to think that the al-Qaeda attacks in which he himself had almost died could be excused in light of the wrongs and injustices that some Muslim countries in the Third World had suffered for decades. Would it not have been a form of justice if Jaramillo had arranged for a bomb to be planted in the apartment manager's office or one of the apartment blocks for which he was responsible?

Was violence not the only option left for the desperately poor and the outcasts? Perhaps Bin Laden was, like Don Quixote, a crazy vigilante who had tried to remedy discrimination by throwing his spears at the tallest windmills.

Feliciano Jaramillo, after one hearing and two appeals, was ejected from the country with no compensation. Angelita, frightened, decided to go back to Colombia with him. Moy followed them. Followed her out of love, and him out of solidarity. They settled in Bogotá, and with the savings stolen from the widow, they opened a small legal advice office. For the first few months, Moy spent almost all his time studying Colombian laws and the language. Then he started to attend proceedings and draft documents—complaints, intimations, and letters rogatory—for workers and peasants who had suffered some kind of abuse and come there in search of help. It was an intense time for him. He had the conviction that he was doing something useful for others, felt once again the youthful emotion of loving someone, and he had begun to fulfill those magnificent dreams that had come back to life in New York when he'd met Albert Fergus. He was living in a different country and learning a new language, he'd bought a car he drove at perilous speeds along the badly surfaced roads surrounding the city, he drank *chicha* every night at La Candelaria, a bar where he went with Jaramillo and some of the people he was protecting, and he had even started to consider the possibility of having a child with Angelita.

He now only vaguely remembered the streets of Manhattan and the smell of food— meat, coffee, pastries, mustard—that always hung in the air, but not one day went by on which he did not remember, with deep sorrow, his son Brent and Adriana. Moy always claimed that he had never stopped loving his wife, even during the times when he had been in love, first with Angelita and then with Alicia, the girl he ended up following to Spain. On the contrary, he presented his romantic experience as proof that true love, that love which is held fast by the buttresses life erects, was something ontologically different from frenzied passion. He was able to be in love with Angelita and continue loving Adriana, in the same way that he enjoyed drinking *chicha* at La Candelaria but when he was at home and stayed up reading till the small hours, poured himself a whisky.

Although many years were yet to pass before Brandon Moy's story concluded, it was in Bogotá that the disillusionment began. He knew from the outset that Angelita's love would be fragile and perishable; he was twenty years older than her, and they formed part of different natures, antagonistic worlds in which it was impossible to find long-lasting bonds other than the bonds of sexuality. What Moy had not imagined is that through Angelita he would become aware of his own estrangement, the process of disintegration that had been taking place in his life.

One day, after he had been in Bogotá for two months, they took a trip to Lake Guatavita, where, as legend would have it, the gold of El Dorado is to be found. They left the car at the end of the road and followed a trail on foot up to the edge of the summit, where the tree-covered slopes of the crater and the colossal fissure that the Spanish conquerors had dug into one side to drain water and lay bare the fabulous treasures could be seen. The scenery was so breathtaking that Moy felt a kind of animal spirituality and wanted to tear off Angelita's clothes in the midst of the vegetation, but just when he was about to do it, some young people appeared on the path, descending from the summit and singing as they came. Angelita blushed as she watched them and then suddenly began to call out and head toward them, overjoyed as she finished fastening the buttons Moy had tried to undo.

There were two boys and three girls the same age as Angelita, whom she knew from Santa Marta, the Caribbean city where she'd been working before leaving to follow Feliciano to Boston. Two of them, Felipe and Rosalinda, had gotten married and now lived in Bogotá. The others had come to visit them for a few days and were doing some sightseeing around the region. Angelita, exhilarated, suggested that they go back to the city together and all have dinner at her house—some *tamales*, *empanadas*, and *patacones*. They would buy beer and wine to celebrate. She didn't consult Moy about the get-together, but when she had recovered from her excitement, she introduced him to her friends adoringly. "This is my American sweetheart," she said. "He's a real handsome gentleman."

Whilst they dined that night, the group of friends recalled old times and talked about people Moy didn't know. Angelita asked them about friends and family members she hadn't seen again since she'd left for the United States, and they couldn't stop talking, telling her how everything was going in Santa Marta and the events and miracles that had taken place recently. Moy, without saying a word, watched them laughing and reminiscing about anecdotes and amusing situations from the past. He was seated apart, behind one of the armchairs in the living room, observing like a meticulous taxonomist wanting to capture everything. He slowly started to realize that as he witnessed Angelita expressing that innocent joy, she was a different creature, a woman he did not know. But when they finished dinner, tipsy from the alcohol, one of the young men, Ramiro, suggested playing a game they apparently used to have fun with when they met up in their free time in Santa Marta. All the others enthusiastically went along with the idea. Angelita ran off to get a pack of cards and found a radio station that played dance music. They sat in a circle around the table, forcing Moy to take part, and distributed the cards. The way the game worked was simple— the players who had the least number of points in their hand had to dance together to the music that was playing at that moment on the radio. The others rated them and then, after deliberating, decided who had been the worst performer. The person chosen had to take off an item of clothing. Then the cards were dealt again.

Moy didn't have bad luck. He had to dance with one of the girls, with Ramiro, and with Angelita. He only got voted off on one occasion and had to remove a shoe. Angelita didn't fair so well and ended the evening in her underwear, like Felipe, who was the overall loser.

Seeing the laughter and satisfaction this mischievous game provoked, with its crazy, adolescent amusement, Moy suddenly felt weighed down by the years, the heaviness that had been gradually piling on with age to detach him from everything. Hypnotized, he stared at Angelita's mouth, her unrestrained peals of laughter, the faces she pulled, like those of an unwitting child who still takes things lightheartedly. That night he had a hunch that it was now too late to try to experience the adventures he had passed up when he was young. He started to think he felt nostalgia for something that couldn't be recovered. And the strangest and most incomprehensible thing was that it wasn't painful to have missed out on life in that way.

From that day on, he couldn't stop looking at Angelita through glasses tinted by this idea. Her impetuosity, her zeal, and her euphoria seemed increasingly ridiculous to him. Sometimes he viewed her with compassion, the way one looks at young people who believe in impossible miracles and utopias that will never come to pass. Moy even found her carnal gestures of love, which were impassioned and affectionate, annoying and unconvincing, the dramatic exaggeration of that which does not last. Some days he got bored. He liked to go for walks around Bogotá, climb up Mount Monserrate, and spend time there taking in the grayish view of the city, the leaden sky that domed it all the way to the horizon. He often remembered Cavafy's poem—"You won't find a new country, won't find another shore. This city will always pursue you." The landscape that could be seen from the mountain—low-rise houses with a few nondescript, misshapen skyscrapers—looked nothing like New York. The climate was completely different—no biting cold or burning heat, and the air lay stagnant, like in a quicksand marsh. There were different smells—heartier stews, groves, moist wood, and trash. Moy was certain when he gazed at the calm, sometimes sleepy rooftops of Bogotá that despite what Cavafy said, there were other countries and other shores, and that life, being so very short, could only be rewarding if one devoted oneself to discovering them.

Moy spent several years going against his own instincts, believing that there was some lost paradise he had to search for (the paradise of Albert Fergus, of his youth) and sensing that it was now too late to do so. He made an effort to behave like Angelita, closing his eyes and laughing in the face of just about anything, casting off the disillusionment he was suffering, but sometimes he couldn't find a way to escape from himself. In those moments, he went to Mount Monserrate, or if it was nighttime, he went for a walk through one of the city's bustling neighborhoods. It was on one of those days, as he came out of a bar in Chapinero where he had been drinking more than usual, that he came across a man who stared at him and made an obscene gesture with his lips. Moy stopped, turned to face him, and felt an urge to hit him, but he stayed still. The man smiled and gave him a cigarette.

"Do you want to come along?" he asked him.

He was a little younger than Moy and had a tattoo on his neck. Moy, feeling dizzy with drunkenness, had the absurd thought that this individual with the sallow face of a hoodlum was the messenger sent by Providence to enable him to satisfy his whims. Without saying a word, he nodded and began to walk behind the man. He was holding the unlit cigarette in his hand. They turned off the avenue on which they had met and wandered for quite a while. The man who was leading the way turned around from time to time to check that Moy was still following him. Finally they arrived at a dingy building with badly worn paintwork. They climbed up to the third floor and went into the man's apartment. It was clean and tidy. There were curtains on the windows and two abstract paintings hanging on the walls. The man turned on a small lamp that gave off a dim light, and then he looked for something in a drawer. He offered Moy a pill.

"You'll feel a lot better with this," he said.

"What is it?" asked Moy, but before the man had time to answer, he whisked it out of his fingers and stuffed it into his mouth.

"Are you foreign?" the man inquired with surprise.

"Give me a whisky," Moy asked. The man gave him a glass of water.

"Better with this," he said.

While Moy drank, the man knelt in front of him and undid his fly. Despite his drunkenness, Moy got an erection immediately. Straightaway, he began to confuse the effects of the blow job with those of the drug he had just taken. He felt a strange sensation of pleasure that was slowly turning into revulsion, but he did not move away, instead he continued obeying the obscene instructions he was receiving—he wetted the man's exposed anus with saliva and straddled him, penetrating him savagely. At the same time as the sexual crescendo was making him dizzy, he could feel nausea in his stomach. He raised his hands squeamishly so as not to touch the man, and after ejaculating, when he withdrew his penis and saw it was dirty with brownish stains, he hurriedly searched for the bathroom in order to vomit. Then he washed himself furiously, as though he were trying to strip off his skin, and went home without saying anything.

The first thing he felt when he got to the street was joy—he had participated in an act that had been thoroughly astonishing and disturbing. It didn't matter whether it had left him happy or disgusted; it boasted the spirit of exaltation, the intensity of epic deeds, it was the kind of chance happening for which he envied Albert Fergus and all those who, according to his assumptions, had dared to confront life with courage. The main character in my book

Woman in Darkness, who only possesses a few vague characteristics of Brandon Moy's psyche, repeats in one particular chapter something he told me one day: "Life is only worth living to excess." What took place in Chapinero was exactly that—the very essence of excess that Moy needed in order to continue believing he had done the right thing in leaving New York.

Moy would have ended up leaving Bogotá sooner or later, since for sometime he hadn't found anything extraordinary or exciting there, and the love of Angelita, whom he now viewed apprehensively, as if she were a child he had to care for instead of a woman with whom he shared a bed, was no longer sufficient to tie him to the city. But there was another painful disappointment that precipitated events. He discovered that Feliciano Jaramillo was taking individuals to his office who, feigning helplessness and reporting abuses that had never taken place, tried to take advantage of his legal advice and skills to make an unjust gain. Jaramillo had come up with an underhanded scheme for attracting clients that involved offering certain day laborers the chance to obtain substantial compensation from their employers if they reported them with fictitious accusations. They made the accusations, Moy prepared the legal arguments, Jaramillo offered the employers a deal in exchange for halting the process, the employers paid to avoid getting a bad reputation, and the money was finally split behind Moy's back between the perjured laborers and Jaramillo, who demanded a commission for the swindle. When an employer proudly refused to pay the settlement, the accusation was withdrawn before trial to prevent the setup being discovered in court. That was what had made Moy suspicious—there were too many cases that were unjustifiably discontinued, too much backpedaling, and, moreover, all in cases with a very similar profile. Moy went warily to see a food industry business owner who had been accused by one of his employees of making him work in conditions of slavery. The business owner denied the accusations and showed Moy documents that evidenced his integrity. Moy distrusted him, but one month later, he went to see the owner of a textile factory, who, describing the same circumstances, proclaimed his innocence and explained the intimidation to which he had been subjected. The third interview took place with a hotel director. Then Moy, having learned his lesson, began to investigate, tracing Jaramillo's steps, and he found out everything.

His love for the down-and-outs of the world suddenly underwent a radical metamorphosis. It disappeared. The al-Qaeda vigilantes became murdering outlaws. Che Guevara, the Colombian guerillas of the FARC, and the indigenous people of Chiapas, whose causes he had sympathized with, transformed into mere criminals, common bandits who stole from others what they were not capable of earning for themselves. He cursed all the romantic ideals that had captivated him since he left the United States and even some other—less noble—ones that he had stood up for throughout his life. He packed in a few hours and after blowing the whistle on Jaramillo and writing Angelita a sentimental letter of goodbye, he departed Bogotá.

Brandon Moy's darkest and most disturbed period followed that moment. He often spoke about it, of the aberrations and excesses in which he indulged, but he always did so in a broad-brush manner, without entering into graphic detail or troubling himself with dates or descriptions. I never found out, for example, what his financial machinations were during those years, where he obtained an income in order to survive, and although he apparently spent a long time living as a hermit without luxuries or conveniences, going from one place to another with a small suitcase in which he kept only the bare essentials, there is no doubt he needed money for his adventures. As well as the costs of food and accommodation, he had to buy the gas for the car he'd bought in Colombia and used to undertake his journey along poorly surfaced roads at reckless speeds.

In Panama it seems he had a fight, which left him with a scar from a knife wound. In Costa Rica he met a group of young Americans and went deep into the rainforest with them for several days to explore nature. In Nicaragua his car almost got stolen, and in Guatemala the police arrested him for reckless driving. Then he crossed Mexico from south to north and finally settled on the outskirts of Hermosillo, where, overnight, he began to do all those things he had attempted throughout his life to hold in check or had only tried in moderation. He became addicted to peyote and its derivatives, he started to drink rum and absinthe without restraint, and he seduced four women with whom he simultaneously maintained, for almost a year, even more tangled marital relations than he had done in Boston. He learned how to ride a horse, shoot a rifle, and play the marimba, a Mexican percussion instrument similar to a xylophone. He read dozens of books and wrote the visionary poems that were subsequently compiled in one volume and merited the praise of critics around the world. He gave saxophone recitals in one of Hermosillo's cantinas. He studied Spanish, Portuguese, and Italian, although he only ended up speaking the first of them fluently. He took part in scuba diving competitions held in the Gulf of California and became an expert in the region's marine life. He set up a small company that organized trips in hot air balloons around the area. And he got a tattoo on his back, spanning from his shoulder blades to the base of his spine, in the form of a snake with its wings spread wide.

"That was me," he explained the day he showed it to me, "a snake with plumage, or a huge eagle with the body of a reptile. A mythological animal, a crossbreed of ill-matched creatures. A being with two natures that doesn't know which one to choose. That was me," he repeated. "Or maybe it still is."

Brandon Moy experienced a feeling of sinister elation throughout those years. Life, which right up until then had always appeared to him as a serene trance and somewhat tedious, now seemed like a process of falling to pieces, or a stampede. The streets of New York were now only a faded, tepid memory, one of those hazy landscapes in which everything seems unreal. Brent's face, in the photo he still possessed, left him cold, indifferent, just like the feeling that certain literary characters leave us with; although we come to love them, we know perfectly well they do not exist. On many nights, he would sit staring at the sky from the back patio of the large, ramshackle house where he lived, trying to understand what exactly happiness was. He never managed to find out, but his investigation enabled him to write some poems, almost theological in nature, of great beauty.

Although it took him time to understand it, the disappointment he had suffered in Bogotá signified the end of his escape. Everything that happened afterward, including his life in Madrid, was an exuberant culmination of what he had imagined he had to do, not of what he really desired. His overindulgence never completely satiated him. Every time he took a step off the straight and narrow, he wanted to take another that would lead him even further astray, so that satisfaction was forever yet another step away. Speed became his great passion. Almost everyday, he would go out on the road and drive for hours, straining the engine to its limits. Sometimes he took part in illegal races held on busy freeways, and even if he didn't win, the physical risk and the nearness of death evoked in him a feeling of vivacious excitement. In those moments, just as when he ejaculated inside a woman, he felt a sensation of immortality and bliss that soothed him. He forgot about all the failures. He forgot about all the things he had never done.

In one of those car races, he had an accident that almost cost him his life. His car swerved off the road, hurtled uncontrollably across a field, and then overturned several times. He ended up face down in the middle of the meadow. He didn't have any spectacular or bloody injuries, but he remained in a coma for eleven days, and the doctors began to think he wouldn't regain consciousness. Two of his female companions took turns sitting up with him in the hospital and caring for him. When he awoke, something surprising happened—he could not remember anything about his new life. He insisted his name was Brandon Moy and didn't understand why everyone was calling him Albert Tracy. He was able to talk to the nurses in Spanish, but he had no memory of Hermosillo, nor did he recognize the women at the foot of his bed.

Little by little he began to recover his memories and reconstruct the years he had spent away from New York. This experience of rebirth or restitution generates a feeling of relief in those who, like him, have suffered amnesia following a head injury, but in Moy it caused a terrible depression. It was like going back to Manhattan and seeing the towers in flames again. He once more remembered the injured woman he'd carried in his arms to a first-aid station. He remembered the futile attempts he had made to speak to Adriana to tell her he was alive. He remembered the moment when he'd placed his cell phone on the pavement and stamped on it wildly to break it to pieces. Finally, he remembered everything that had happened afterward—the journey in the truck to Boston, stealing the purse, working at the coffee shop, Daisy's love and the love of the wealthy lady, Angelita's body, the views from Mount Monserrate, the beaches of Nicaragua, and at the end of the road, the barren terrain on which the car had spun out of control before beginning to flip over in the air. He remembered all of it as if it had happened to someone else, as though it were a fable or a parable he wasn't quite able to interpret. He even recalled all the dreams he'd had the night of September 10, when he'd bumped into Albert Fergus and thought about his youth. He knew, therefore, what his reasoning had been at that moment and the logical process he had followed to make his decisions. But despite that, he was not capable of understanding why he had walked away from his old life. It seemed strange to him, inexplicable, like those behaviors that are alien to our nature and when we see them in others, we can never fully comprehend.

When he finished his convalescence, he locked himself away to write poems and letters he almost always tore up before mailing. He sent one, though, to Laureen, the wife of the Italian diplomat whom he'd met in Boston, and she replied. They kept up a romantic (or, more precisely, erotic) correspondence for some months, and when Moy completed his book, he sent it to her; she was the only person in whose artistic sensibility he trusted. Laureen was impressed and immediately sent it to Richard Palfrey, who got in touch with Moy straightaway to offer to publish it. Moy had his doubts. He didn't know if the book should be signed by Albert Tracy, he didn't know which one of the two had created it. In the end, perhaps goaded by the vanity of becoming a writer, which was something he had wanted to do for so many years, he accepted. He moved to Saltillo, near Monterrey, and subsequently to

Mexico City, where he undertook a variety of menial jobs. When "The City" with Albert Tracy's signature was finally published and highly favorable reviews began to appear in the most reputable literary circles, the Universidad Nacional Autónoma invited him to join them as a visiting lecturer and give a seminar on American poetry. It was during that time that I met him.

Due to the labyrinth that his memory and his life had become, Moy transformed into an almost mystical figure. He grew a beard, which was peppered with gray hair even though he wasn't that old, and he developed the habit of speaking in a very quiet tone of voice, like missionaries or spiritual advisors. He once again became interested in the dispossessed, and he worked on several educational support projects that operated in the slums and small towns on the outskirts of the city. He responded to his literary success with elusiveness, since he was afraid someone seeing his face in photos might recognize him. He stopped writing and rejected many offers to attend congresses and literary fairs. He also declined most of the interviews the newspapers and television channels requested, although in so doing he only managed to boost his fame, since people began to compare his mysterious secrecy with that of Thomas Pynchon, Bruno Traven, or J. D. Salinger.

Moy turned into a somber, distracted man. He no longer tried to fulfill those impetuous, extravagant desires he had listed in a notebook years earlier. He didn't even remember them. He lived an orderly, monotonous life. He read a lot, prepared his university classes, visited the neighborhood educational missions, gave legal advice to a nongovernmental organization, went for walks through the city, and watched films on television. He had begun to sense, as though he were converting to Buddhism, that happiness did not lie in fulfilling desires but rather in not having any. That's why for several months he even abstained from women and underwent a period of chastity. But willpower is not enough to steer the course of life, as he himself wrote, with greater refinement, in one of his poems— "The facts are never enough for life,"—and after a time, he fell in love again.

Alicia hailed from Madrid and was in Mexico collaborating with an indigenous political action group. She was twenty-seven and still believed in the revolution that would change the world. She lived with other young people in a grubby, shared apartment that didn't even have a bathroom. She was passionate and angry. The first time Moy saw her, she was trying to hit a school security guard who was almost twelve inches taller than her and who would have been able to flatten her with a single blow. That innocuous, untamable rage touched him. He went to protect her and ended up confronting the security guard himself. He then realized that Alicia was very attractive and that it was impossible to live without ever taking risks. Sensing the same gleeful disappointment with which someone who's on the wagon succumbs to the temptation of drinking once again, Moy got slowly back into the swing of things. He felt outrage and affection again. He felt pain, sorrow, and sensuality. Without forethought, without knowing exactly what was happening, he started to make plans with Alicia and commit himself to her.

Although we hadn't spoken again since the writers' congress in Cuernavaca at which we met, Moy wrote me a lengthy letter and then called to break the news that he was coming to live in Madrid with Alicia. She was the daughter of a multimillionaire construction company owner, and although she displayed that violent rebellion against authority and conventions to which Moy had been witness, she always had the financial support of her family. This unseemly contradiction made Alicia more attractive in Moy's eyes, since in a warped way, he found in her the same need to break away from everything that had urged him to leave New York. Weary of the discomforts of Mexico and her philanthropic work, she decided to return to Madrid, where her father offered her a small apartment in a working class area so that she could hold onto her pride. There was nothing to keep Moy in Mexico, and having often dreamed of seeing Europe, he followed her.

In his letter he explained that he didn't know anyone in Madrid and that he would like to see me. I offered to help him with whatever he needed and invited him to a party I throw every summer on the rooftop terrace of my house, so that he could meet some of my writer friends and enter the city's literary circles. At the party, I introduced him to, amongst others, Marta Sanz, Javier Montes, and Marcos Giralt, all of whom he saw frequently during the following months. Nonetheless, the closest relationship he formed was with Fernando Royuela, since both had a certain propensity for abstract conversation, ambiguous speculation, and political spiritualism. Royuela read Moy's book of poetry with admiration, and Moy, who found it difficult to understand Royuela's polished, cosmogonical prose in Spanish, ended up being fascinated by his novels.

Straightaway, I became the person he trusted in Madrid. I went with him to sort out some red tape, I took him to visit Toledo and the Prado Museum, and although Alicia's father also provided him with money, I got him several translation jobs for informational books that a publishing house I worked with at that time was going to release. Perhaps because he, like me, had a wistful and somewhat disconsolate nature, we became friends instantly. He would drop by the office some afternoons to pick me up, and we would go out for beers in the bars around Argüelles. We always started off talking about literature, politics, or impersonal matters, but little by little, as the effects of the alcohol began to relax us, we would give free rein to our confessions and tell each other all the indiscretions that crossed our minds.

On one of those days, during a drunken conversation, he disclosed to me that he was not called Albert Tracy but rather Brandon Moy and that he had previously had another life. We were in a small bar on the Calle Gaztambide, seated at a table. There were a lot of people at the bar drinking and celebrating. Suddenly, Moy began to sob and started talking about his wife and son without giving me any prior explanations. His speech slurring due to the alcohol, he then told me everything that had taken place on September 11, 2001, after the Twin Towers had been razed to the ground. Going back and forth in time, as if he were telling one of those experimental tales in which the chronology is jumbled, he described his life in New York before the disaster, the dreams he'd had as a young man, the promises he'd made to Adriana when they had married, the professional disappointments, and the plans he'd had for his son. He also remembered in great detail the conversation with Albert Fergus outside the Continental restaurant, Tracy's laughter, and the motion picture image of the taxi driving away through the streets of Manhattan. He was speaking for over an hour. He only stopped to go up to the bar and collect the beers he had ordered by signaling at the waiter. On a few occasions, he lost the thread of the story and sat staring into space as though he were miles away. But then, after a few seconds, his eyes began to gleam again, and finding some link in his memory, he continued relating his story pitifully.

"There are things that should only be achievable when we want them for the first time," he said to me in a hoarse, cracking voice. "Continuing to desire them afterward is a tragedy. Above all, it's a mirage."

We sat in silence for a while, rolling our empty glasses on the table. Then I suddenly remembered a story about a couple in love who, a century before Moy, had tried to stray from their destiny. In a rather ill-judged way, I started to recount it, as if in so doing, I were trying to offer him some consolation.

"I once heard about some young people from Barcelona who went through the opposite of what happened to you," I began. "They were rich, part of the Catalonian bourgeoisie that built empires at the beginning of this past century. They decided to get married and insisted on spending their honeymoon in New York. At their age, they thought the city was paradise. They dreamed of jazz clubs, lavish hotels, enormous skyscrapers, and a world of high society that didn't exist in Europe. But their families must have held all the archaic convictions of their ancestry, and they refused to agree to the extravagant trip. Why did they have to go to New York when Vienna or Paris were more elegant and decent than that faraway

American city known only for its lewd, modern lifestyle and the depraved acts that went on there?"

Despite being drunk, I immediately realized the story only contained a few absurd coincidences with that of Moy. He looked at me with his eyes wide, and still teary, but I don't know if he was listening to me.

"The stubborn couple planned everything in secret. They pretended they were going to obey the sensible wishes of their parents and travel with their butler to Paris, where they had a hotel booked for two months. Once there, in Paris, they bribed the butler to send a postcard everyday to each of their families, and then they went straight on to Southampton, where a luxury ocean liner everyone was talking about was going to set sail for New York. On the tenth of April, 1912, they boarded the *Titanic*, delighted to have managed to outwit the moldy prejudices of their social class. Four days later, the ship sank and they died. The butler, in a state of panic over his disloyalty in betraying his real employers, continued sending postcards to the families throughout the two months the couple was supposed to be staying in Paris. He didn't want to lose his job. Or didn't want to feel the shame of his deceit. Perhaps he came to believe there could've been a miracle and the young lovers would come back from the dead. In the postcards, he wrote about luxurious balls, monuments, parties beside the Seine, and trips to Versailles. The couple's parents continued imagining their children were happy for those two months."

I stopped speaking and got up to get two more beers. When I returned to the table, Moy was still motionless, staring straight ahead at the body of air occupying the place where I had been.

"What happened then?" he asked when I had sat down again.

I took a sip of beer and shrugged my shoulders. I wasn't sure what it was that Moy wanted to know.

"The butler went to live in New York," I improvised. "And perhaps from there he kept sending the odd postcard."

That day, when he told me his story, Brandon Moy had already begun his moral collapse. He had been living in Madrid for about six months, and for weeks the only thing that was binding him to Alicia was the erotic savagery he continued feeling when he saw her naked. He couldn't bear her inconsistency, like that of a spoilt child, or her unpredictable outbursts of rage. He was planning to leave her, rent an apartment, and live alone, but his finances wouldn't allow it, and at his age (he had just turned forty-eight), he didn't feel up to looking for a new job. He had started drinking too much and living a completely chaotic life. It was during this time when the versions he gave of his past, paradoxical and sometimes incoherent, changed from one day to the next. One night he claimed that when leaving New York he had been happy and had found the intensity and passion he had been pursuing, and the following night, either more drunk or more sober, he would start to cry wretchedly and admit that in all those years, he had never stopped thinking about Adriana and missing the streets of Manhattan.

On one of those days of nostalgia, it occurred to Moy to step up to the brink of the abyss—he turned on Alicia's computer to go into Adriana's email account and read her messages. Moy remembered perfectly the email address his wife had used for years for her personal correspondence. There was a chance she might have closed the account after he left New York, but if not, Moy could log onto it and spy on her, find out if she had a lover or even if she had remarried, whether she was still in touch with the same friends, if Brent had grown up unscathed. His hands trembling with fear, he typed in the email address and a random password. The system responded that the password was incorrect and asked him if he had forgotten it. Moy clicked Yes, and the ever-agile system offered him three options for recovering the forgotten password: receive a link in another of Adriana's email accounts (the one she used for work) to restore it; receive a verification code on the cell phone associated with the account, which also belonged to Adriana; or reply to a security question. Moy clicked on the last option, the only one that could pry open the gate, and waited for a few more seconds before clicking again. When he did so, the system showed the security question he had to answer, the question that Adriana had entered at some point to guarantee her secrets were safe—"What part of my body is blue?"

Brandon Moy began to weep profusely for a long while. Then, breathless, his sight still completely blurred with tears, he typed in the response. In New York it was early morning, so Adriana would be asleep. Moy went through all the steps and finally got into the email account. He felt a kind of swelling at the top of his throat, choking him—the horror of discovering something dreadful, on the one hand, and the vicious act of violating that which should be secret. There were more than three hundred messages that had been sent or received by Adriana in the last eight months. Moy spent several hours opening them one by one. In all of them, he found the insignificance he was hoping for, the banality of unimportant affairs—a dental appointment, a dinner invitation from Marion and Frank, a notice for a college counseling meeting for Brent, a reminder of household chores, notes on recipes exchanged with friends, insubstantial, light-hearted, vague messages.

He turned off the computer with an almost religious sense of sin, of guilt without redemption, although not because of having infringed Adriana's privacy, rather for having taken his own life to the limits of devastation and wreckage. Perhaps, that day, he began to think that the land he had left behind was not altogether parched, that it might still contain some fertile soil. He recalled once again the men who had thrown themselves from the towers of the World Trade Center, fleeing from the flames, and asked himself whether they had been capable, during the seconds it took to fall, of thinking that something could save them before they smashed into the ground. Whether they had been capable of believing that their lives could begin again.

Although we saw each other fairly regularly, Moy and I did not have a fixed routine or see each other on a weekly basis, so when some time passed without hearing from him, I wasn't surprised. When I called him at home and Alicia, to whom I preferred not to speak, answered, I would hang up without saying anything. One day, I unexpectedly received a postcard he had sent me from Italy. It bore a picture of the Pantheon in Rome. It didn't include a return address or any precise information about his journey, and it didn't offer any justification for his departure. He had only scrawled one phrase, in thick letters, in English. "It's always the same city, but sometimes the roads are more beautiful." It was signed Brandon Moy, which was a forewarning (that I was not able to grasp) of what was to come.

In Italy he was living with Laureen, first in Rome in the diplomat's house, and then in Orvieto, Florence, Bologna, Milan, and Venice, where she, having secured her elderly husband's acquiescence to her maintaining a discreetly licentious life, accompanied him. As in Boston, she was his Pygmalion. She showed him cathedrals and paintings, she unveiled the secrets of Buonarroti to him and taught him about the turbulent history of the Medici and Visconti families. She made him sample Italian wines and took him to see the famous landscapes of the Tuscan countryside. It was a long holiday during which Moy, as though it were his swan song, a recapitulation of everything, finally found himself. He sent me other postcards, which I still have, but in none of them after that first one from Rome were there any signs of his intentions. In Pisa, he told me of the beauty of the Arno river; in Florence, of Dante's Inferno and the ugliness of Petrarca; in Venice, of Igor Stravinski, buried in the San Michele cemetery; and in Turin, of the Italian women, whom, because of Laureen, he had not been able to get to know in any depth.

One day, when I was leaving the office, he was waiting for me outside. We hadn't seen each other for about four or five months, and he hadn't informed me of his arrival. He was wearing a new, black wool coat that caught my attention because it gave him such an elegant look. I had never seen such refinement from him. Also, his face seemed to have changed; he was neatly shaved and had a haircut that highlighted his features and made him look younger. His expression was serene, confident. He was smiling, and as soon as he saw me step outside, he came to embrace me.

That day, Brandon Moy had come to a decision and he wanted to tell me about it. He had returned to Madrid three days earlier and was staying in a modest hotel with the money Laureen had lent him.

"I could have married Laureen," he told me, laughing as we walked toward one of the bars where we usually got together. "The ambassador doesn't have many years left in him, and she needs to keep doing crazy things with someone."

He asked me to call my house to check that no one was expecting me for dinner and started to explain, between touristic descriptions of Italy and anecdotes about the journey, what his plan was. He had arrived in Spain more than a year ago, and almost three years had passed since he'd had his accident in Hermosillo. During all that time that he'd been fettered firstly by the shadows of death and then by the charms of Alicia's or Laureen's love, Moy had slowly realized that nothing that had happened in Boston, Bogotá, Mexico, or Madrid had made him happy. All those dreams he had fulfilled as though they had been part of a ceremony— the peyote deliria, the promiscuity, the hot air balloon trips, the diving feats—had never ended up satiating him, because in reality he had neither felt any particular fascination for them nor taken any pleasure in them; on the contrary, he had experienced displeasure. He'd pursued them because he'd always believed that through these things, he would get to know the essence of the world. Since childhood he had heard it said that the real core of life was to be found in danger, in excess, in a pushing of limits, or indulgence. In a constant state of flux. Those who sedately went to the office everyday, were faithful to their spouses, watched television at night, and always went to the same places each year on vacation were obscure, nonexistent beings. Specters that leave no prints on anything they touch. That was the law, the commandment—one had to seek out recklessness, since order and calm lead only to death.

Brandon Moy did not call that law into question, but he was beginning to realize that it had not been decreed for him. He remembered dispassionately all the times he had gone astray during the last few years, and he understood that he was one of those obscure beings who are only soothed by insubstantiality, one of those men with a leaden, gray spirit. He missed his wife, and some days, when making love to Alicia or Laureen, he had to think about her to become sexually aroused. Perhaps he would never be happy in Manhattan, living in a sunny house, doing an exhausting, thankless job, and disappointedly watching his son grow up, but now he was certain he would be unhappy anywhere else.

"Royuela told me Cavafy's story, which he himself had written at some point," he said as he drank. "He was born in Alexandria, and on his father's death, when he was still a child, he moved with his family to England, where he was raised and learned English, which was the first language in which he tried to write poetry. Then he lived in Constantinople and spent periods of time in London, France, and Athens. But he wanted to return to Alexandria and live there working at a dull job in a government office reporting to the Department of Public Works."

"The city," I said.

"The city," he nodded, and then, after clearing his throat, he began to recite. " 'You will walk the same streets, grow old in the same neighborhoods, will turn gray in these same houses.' "

I remained quiet for a few seconds. Moy was about to cry.

"Are you going to go back?"

He didn't say anything. He drained the glass of the wine he was drinking, and with very slow movements, as though he wanted to give himself one last chance to change his mind, he searched in one of his pants pockets and took out a coin, which he placed on the table, directly in front of me. It was fifty cents.

"Once, a few days after leaving, I was about to call Adriana to tell her I was alive and I was going to go back to New York. I didn't do it, because something happened, but I kept the coin not knowing why. Now I know."

He had already told me that story—the desperation he had felt in Boston, the need to steal to afford a night's sleep in a warm bed, the fear, the woman who'd crossed his path, the bills that were in the purse he'd snatched from her, the satisfaction of that danger.

"It's fifty U.S. cents," I said to him unthinkingly, as though creating an allegory. "You can't call from a phone in Spain with that coin."

Moy smiled and shrugged his shoulders, indifferent to symbolism.

"Swap me for a euro, will you. I'll get the beers."

"I'll miss you," I said, not really sure that it was true.

He looked at me gratefully and stretched out his hand on the table to squeeze mine, but he couldn't reach between the glasses, and the action turned into a clumsy, hurried gesture.

"'This city will always pursue you,'" he said.

That day, after getting drunk with me and confessing the sorrow that had wracked him since he left New York, Moy went to his hotel, staggering with drunkenness and remorse, and sat down to write a lengthy account of his wayward years, as he himself referred to them, in order to be sure that what he was going to do was, this time, without any doubt, the right thing. In this account, he told the absolute truth—that he was not called Albert Tracy, that he was a real estate lawyer who had a wife and child, that he had always lived in New York and had fled from there on the day when the al-Qaeda planes smashed into the World Trade Center. He mentioned Albert Fergus and the dreams they had shared when they were young. His literary ambitions, the countries he intended to visit some day, the women he had charmed with his vivid imaginings and boasting. He explained, quite unashamedly, as if it were an act of atonement, that he had never truly loved (although he had been convinced that he had) Angelita, Alicia, and all those women who had made his heart swell with fantasies, and that all the affairs he'd had over the last few years since he'd left New York had only caused him angst and fear. Lastly, he admitted that he wanted to go home and see his friends again. Spend weekends on Long Island, go swimming on 51st Street, and have meetings with construction companies at the top of skyscrapers, where the empty rooftops of his city could be seen. "This is my nature, and I cannot change it," he wrote as dawn began to break. "When serpents shed their skin, there appears below another, which is just the same, with the same patterns and the same cold, clammy cuticle. It could not live, even if it wished to, in the skin of a deer or the feathers of an eagle."

Then he took off his clothes and, twisting his neck, looked at his back in the closet mirror. He tried to touch it with the tips of his fingers. He thought he should remove the eagle wings from the serpent in his tattoo.

Moy devoted the following days to packing up his things. He prepared his luggage in a disciplined manner, bought a plane ticket to New York, and said goodbye to me and all his Spanish friends. He traveled to Chicago on Thursday, January 8, and went through customs with the fake Albert Tracy passport. From there, he called Adriana with the fifty-cent coin and told her a convoluted, unoriginal story that she, thrilled by his resurrection, nonetheless believed without hesitation. He told her that on the day of the attacks, he had lost consciousness and completely forgotten who he was, that he had walked aimlessly for weeks and traveled through strange towns and unfamiliar cities until he ended up in Chicago, where he'd been living ever since. Now, at last, with the help of a psychiatrist and the healing that always comes with time, he remembered everything. Many years had passed since that September day, and perhaps she, Adriana, had met another man and had fallen in love again, but if by any chance that was not so and she still had something of the love she had for him in the past, Moy could go to New York that very night and remain by her side forever. It took Adriana a while to answer, since her sobbing prevented her from being able to speak. When she calmed down, she assured him blatheringly that she had never stopped thinking about him and would never be able to love another man. They talked for over two hours. Then Moy caught the first flight for New York and was reunited with her.

I only saw Brandon Moy again one more time, when I was in Manhattan in June 2010, but we've spoken on the phone several times and regularly send each other emails and even postcards, so I'm abreast of what's happening in his life. They let him return to the company he worked at prior to the attacks, and a few months later, he was promoted. He went on vacation with Adriana to Italy and pretended to discover with her the beauty of the Sistine Chapel and the majesty of the Basilica of Saint Mary of the Flower. He took his son, who was now a teenager, camping in the Catskill Mountains. He was never able to have dinner at the Continental, which closed its doors shortly after he'd left, but he often goes out with Adriana to fashionable bars and is well acquainted with Manhattan high society, the art exhibitions, the clubs, and the literary festivals. His life is very similar to his old one, but now he views it with a different kind of discernment. "I'm not happy, but at least now I know that I can't ever be," he wrote in a letter he sent me at Christmas 2011. "There is no uncertainty, and that, in my opinion, is a form of happiness."

The poet Albert Tracy, who had stirred up so much excitement among a number of critics in the United States, disappeared without a trace. He didn't publish anymore books, attend any conferences or poetry gatherings, but it seems nobody missed him, perhaps because readers and literary scholars are used to transience and fickleness. At that time, I was the only person, along with the Australian girl in Boston and Alicia, who knew the truth about his disappearance, and I wrote an article, in a legendary tone, in which I reviewed his limited biography and his foolhardy, secret life, comparing him with some of the great poets who had achieved glory through seclusion and mystery.

Many months after all this happened, I also decided to write a fictional story inspired by the adventures of Brandon Moy. I had intended to change the names and some of the more incidental circumstances, but the essence of the story was going to be identical to the real one. I made notes, as I always do, drafted a few speculative reflections about identity and the meaning of life, collected some photographs of the places where Moy had been, and read books and records about the September 11 attacks to familiarize myself with it all. Glancing over a report I found online about the planes that were hijacked that day, I saw by chance a name that astounded me and convinced me once and for all that Brandon Moy's existence was either a parable or a tall tale—among the passengers on American Airlines Flight 11,which, under the direction of Mohamed Atta, crashed into the North Tower of the World Trade Center, was Albert Fergus. He was returning to Los Angeles from Boston, where he had flown just after running into Moy as he was leaving the Continental.

ABOUT THE AUTHOR

LUISGÉ MARTÍN is a multi-awarded Spanish writer born in Madrid in 1962. He has published the short story collections *Los oscuros* (1990) *El alma del erizo* (2002) and *Todos los crímenes se cometen por amor* (2013); the collection of correspondence *Amante del sexo busca pareja morbosa* (2002); and the book of travels *Donde el silencio* (2013). Along with *The Same City* and *Woman in Darkness*, published in English by Hispabooks, his novels include *La dulce ira* (1995), *La muerte de Tadzio* (2000)— winner of the Premio Ramón Gómez de la Serna—*Los amores confiados* (2005), *Las manos cortadas* (2009), and his latest release, *La vida equivocada* (2015). He has also worked as an editor for Ediciones SM and in Ediciones del Prado and he contributes occasionally to *El Viajero, Babelia, El País* and other Spanish publications.

ABOUT THE TRANSLATOR

Tomasz Dukanovich is a self-taught Spanish-English translator who lives in Madrid. He has had a very varied professional background, having been a pianist, social worker, lawyer and language teacher. As a translator he has mainly specialized in the business and legal fields but has also worked on a wide range of projects going from art, history and philosophy through to psychiatry. Relatively new in the world of literary translation, he is now beginning to work more and more in this area for which he has discovered a real passion.

CPSIA information can be obtained at www.ICGtesting.com
Printed in the USA
LVOW11s1934020815

448542LV00003B/4/P

AUG 3 1 2015¹ ₦ 1495